Dragonfly in the Land of Swamp Dragons

RESA NELSON

ISBN: 153026605X
ISBN-13: 978-1530266050

ACKNOWLEDGEMENTS

As always, many thanks to my fellow authors, Carla Johnson, Tom Sweeney, Frank Stearns, and Rich Bradford for their excellent feedback and suggestions.

RESA NELSON

Also by Resa Nelson

The Dragonslayer Series:

The Dragonslayer's Sword (Book 1)
The Iron Maiden (Book 2)
The Stone of Darkness (Book 3)
The Dragon's Egg (Book 4)

The Dragonfly Series:

Dragonfly (Book 1)
Dragonfly in the Land of Ice (Book 2)

Standalone novels:

Our Lady of the Absolute
All of Us Were Sophie

CHAPTER 1

Questions plagued Greeta while she fed small bits of driftwood into a fire that heated a large shell filled with seawater and clams.

Why can't I remember how to turn into a dragon? Why couldn't I do it when it counted most? I'm the only one who has seen Finehurst's darkest secrets. I'm the only one who knows how dangerous he is. If I'd turned into a dragon earlier today, I could have captured him. I could have protected all of the Great Turtle Lands, and now its people are in danger—just like us.

Frayka and Njall trudged through the fine white sand and dumped large pieces of driftwood next to Greeta.

"We already wasted too much time guiding the ship ashore," Njall said. He pointed at the Northlander ship that he and Frayka had guided onto the beach with the help of the incoming tide. Like all Northlander ships, it sported a low, sleek design in the shape of a fearsome sea dragon. "I still think we should be setting sail for home instead of frittering our time away making fires and gathering wood."

Frayka crossed her arms and squared off to face him. Although she stood as tall as Greeta and Njall, Frayka looked nothing like them. Unlike the blonde and fair people in her Northlander clan, Frayka had black hair and eyes like her grandmother from the Far East. "And let a dangerous sorcerer like Finehurst threaten the world? I think not. Besides, you already promised to stay and help us."

Njall muttered, "Best thing to do is help you change your mind."

Greeta looked up at them, troubled by their bickering.

We wouldn't have these problems if I knew how to turn into a dragon whenever I want! I could have stopped Finehurst by now and we'd be on our way home.

Greeta pointed at the large pieces of driftwood they'd brought. "These are too big for the fire."

"Those aren't for the fire," Erik said. "They're for me."

Even though Erik washed ashore moments ago, the sight of him still startled Greeta. Months ago, she and Frayka met

Erik and his group of Northlander men, who had been dead for many years. The men's spirits inhabited any collection of earthly material they could cobble together into a body.

However, since escaping the Land of Ice, only Erik's head remained, which consisted of black rocks and bits of driftwood packed into a tight ball. Tiny vines with red berries covered his head like hair. "I figure the time has come to pull myself together in a new body." Under his breath he said, "Which wouldn't be necessary had your friend not yanked me from my previous body."

Frayka cleared her throat, turning to look down at Erik's head. "If not for me, you'd still be frozen inside the dragon goddess's castle."

Showing his annoyance, Erik's eyes glowed like embers when he returned her gaze. "At least I'd be with friends."

Frayka scoffed. "Friends just as frozen as you in that ice palace? All of you just standing there, not able to move? Stuck there for who knows how long?"

Erik sniffed. "At least I'd be with good company."

Frayka hiked up her skirt to her knees and lifted one foot, aiming it at Erik.

"Frayka, please," Greeta said. "Not again. It took too long to find him the last time you kicked him into the ocean."

Erik bared his shard-like stony teeth at Frayka.

"None of that," Greeta said, pointing at Erik. "If you bite anyone I'll kick you into the sea myself and no one will swim out to find you next time."

Taking a step toward Erik, Frayka tapped him with the inside of her foot, causing him to roll into the large pieces of driftwood. "That should be enough for a new start. Create yourself anew."

A bubbling sound caught Greeta's attention, and she checked the clams in the boiling seawater. "These will be ready to eat in a while."

Njall took a few steps toward the incoming tide, his expression grave and earnest. "What are we doing here when we have a perfectly good ship? We should be sailing for home." He gestured toward the eastern horizon. "The storm is all but gone."

Joining his side, Greeta looked up to see the skies clearing above. At the same time, a black wall of clouds and rain stood in the distance. The pending storm reminded her of Norah, a water dragon with the power to control all forms of water, whether rain, ice, or mist.

That storm in the distance must be Norah. She's watching us.

"We agreed to help Norah," Greeta said. "We promised to find Finehurst and stop him."

"I didn't," Njall said. "I don't know Finehurst. He has nothing to do with us." Njall gestured to the landscape surrounding them. "If he's here, then let the natives fight him."

"It isn't just about helping Norah," Greeta said. "It's about protecting people, including Northlanders. What if he plans to kill all of us?"

"We don't know what he plans. Not exactly." Njall shook his head. "The best way to protect our people is to go home. We'll tell them about Finehurst. Tell them he's the sorcerer who's been threatening us, but that we drove him away."

"I'm not so sure that's what happened." Greeta kept an eye on the storm in the distance. The dark wall swiveled like an opening door. "And what about the magic he can do with the tapestry?"

Njall laughed. "We have the last piece of that tapestry. Seems to me the tapestry won't do him any good until he gets all the pieces assembled."

Greeta shivered. "But he manipulated us into getting more tapestry pieces for him. We're lucky he didn't get the last one from us already. What if he hurts people who live here or convinces them to hurt us? We have to stop him before it's too late." She swallowed hard. "We need to trap him somewhere so he'll never escape."

"Greeta is wrong," Frayka said. "Trapping him isn't enough. Finehurst must be killed." Frayka strolled toward them, staring at the incoming tide. "But Greeta is also correct. It has to be us. According to the portents."

"The portents?" Njall looked up at her. "What portents? You said nothing about this before."

Frayka gazed at the ocean as if in a trance. When she spoke, her voice drifted like that of an ethereal spirit. "This portent is something new. If we fail, we put our families at risk."

Njall paced. "Are my parents and brothers safe?"

"For now," Frayka said. "But not if you return to the Land of Ice."

The edge of the storm stood in the distance like a sentinel keeping watch.

Njall made no effort to hide his distress. "I'll find more wood." He marched down the beach.

Greeta studied Frayka. "A new portent? When did that happen?"

Frayka gave her a sideways glance and a brief smile. "I haven't decided yet."

Erik walked stiffly on his driftwood legs to stand between the two women. "So Frayka knows how to wrap Njall around her little finger. What else is new?" He looked from one woman to the other. "We should waste no more time. If we don't know where Finehurst has gone and we have no way to track him, how do we find him?"

A sudden clatter distracted them.

Turning in the direction of the sound, Greeta saw a handful of large gulls around her fire. They'd knocked the shell filled with boiling seawater over, dumping the clams on the beach. Steam spilled across the sand. Realizing they'd been found out, the gulls squawked noisily while they stood guard around the hot clams.

"Good," Frayka said. She withdrew her dagger. "Now we can have birds for lunch."

Greeta looked at her in dismay. "We are not killing those birds!"

Frayka returned the same look of dismay. "Did you cook those clams to feed us or those birds?"

Greeta stepped forward and waved her hands at the gulls, but they stood their ground.

Spreading their wings, they snapped at her. One gull gave a steaming clam a tentative poke with its clawed foot, only to discover it was still too hot.

Defeated, Greeta left the gulls alone. "What harm will it do to let the birds have the clams?"

Frayka's expression turned to astonishment. "You look like a Northlander but don't act like one. You are soft and weak!"

"I'm not soft. I'm not weak." Greeta turned her back on the gulls and shrugged. "It's easy to get more clams."

Frayka shook her head in disappointment and tucked her dagger away. "As long as you're the one who digs them up."

Far out at sea, lightning flashed and illuminated the pulsating black storm line. The skies rumbled and cracked. The air smelled strange and fresh.

Returning her attention to it, Greeta said, "See the storm out there?"

Frayka and Erik turned to look at the ocean.

"I'm certain that's Norah," Greeta said. "And I think she will point the way to Finehurst."

Erik looked at the storm. "Finehurst? But the cloud points at us."

CHAPTER 2

A sudden sea breeze cut through the warm air like a shard of ice. Greeta and Frayka shivered.

"What if it isn't?" Greeta said. "What if the cloud points *beyond* us?"

They followed the direction of the storm's extended arm toward the beach behind them and its border of tall grass.

"Look!" Greeta said, pointing at the rivulet of water streaming between the shoreline and the grass line. "It's moving!"

The narrow trench of water running across the width of the beach wriggled like a snake. The hard-packed sand surrounding it cracked and broke apart when the trench shifted its position. Like a living thing, it wrenched itself free from the grass line and crawled alongside that border. Finally, it stopped at a gap in the border where a sandy path appeared to cut through the grass land.

"That's the path we should follow," Greeta said.

Frayka stared at Greeta, her face blank with disbelief. "Are you telling me that dragon goddess is hanging back and keeping her own hide safe while telling us where to go?"

"Makes sense," Erik said. Losing his battle with balance, his new legs tumbled to the sand and his head landed next to them. "Last time she put herself in Finehurst's path he locked her up in her own ice castle for twenty years. She's smart to risk our skins instead of hers. And we do owe her."

Greeta and Frayka turned in unison to stare at Erik.

"Owe her?" Frayka said.

Erik made the sound of clearing his throat even though he had none. "All right, it could be me that owes her." He cleared his non-existent throat again. "Happened after Finehurst killed me and my men. He dragged what was left of us through the Southlands and Midlands and Northlands. Then he promised we'd live again if we helped him get a girl out of a well."

"Norah?" Greeta said.

Erik rolled his head forward slightly to nod. "Finehurst failed to mention the girl was a dragon goddess."

"How did Norah end up in a well?" Frayka said. "What was she doing there?"

"Never understood that," Erik said. "Finehurst said we had one chance to live again. We thought we'd find our families." He heaved a sigh. "None of us knew our families were dead. All we knew was a terrible storm had wrecked the world." He looked up. "Our part of the world, that is."

"You helped Finehurst take Norah from the well, which was probably a safe place for her," Greeta said. She heard the edge in her voice. "And then you took her to the Land of Ice?"

Erik rolled to nod again. "He kept telling us lies about Norah being an evil sorceress who had to be stopped or else she'd kill our families. None of us knew Finehurst had become a sorcerer. Not until he conjured a ship for us to set sail in."

"And he conjured another ship in the Land of Ice," Frayka said. "He must have hidden in the ice castle. That's where we saw him for the first time. Except for Greeta, of course."

"I don't think that was Finehurst," Greeta said.

"Of course it was Finehurst." Frayka pointed at Erik. "Even this dead man recognized him. And so did you!"

"Like I told you before, what we saw wasn't mortal," Greeta said.

"It's Finehurst, and you know it," Frayka said. "Doesn't matter if he's mortal or not. It's him."

Njall joined them, dumping an armful of driftwood next to Erik. "Doesn't matter if who's mortal?"

"Finehurst," Greeta said. "But what matters now is making sure the ship is far enough inland and well hidden before we leave."

Plopping down next to Frayka, Njall said, "Leave? Where are we going?"

"Looking for Finehurst," Frayka said. "Whether he's mortal or not."

"Great," Njall moaned. "Just great."

* * *

After sorting through the new pile of driftwood that Njall gathered, Erik reconstructed himself. He replaced his driftwood legs with branches and stood as tall as Greeta. Erik plodded by her side while they followed the sandy trail. Frayka and Njall lagged behind.

The beach grass flanking the path grew shoulder high and waved in the warm ocean breeze. Greeta felt the heat of the sand through the deerskin soles of her shoes. She watched where she walked. Although far away from the incoming tide, broken shells and dismembered claws poked through the sand.

By the time the sun reached its highest

point, the path opened onto a river. Although they'd all filled their flasks with fresh water they'd found near the beach, Njall ran toward the river. He kneeled on its sandy bank and scooped a handful of water into his mouth but then spat it out.

"What's wrong?" Greeta said.

Njall's face twisted as if the water pained him, and he rinsed his mouth out with water from his flask before he drank. "Salt."

Greeta leaned down to dip her fingertips in the river. Sure enough, the water left them feeling sticky. "This river comes from the ocean."

"Look!" Erik shouted. He pointed upriver at the sea grass on the same bank. A pile of rubble peeked above the tall, spiky grass.

"Erik?" a distant but familiar voice called out.

"Antoni!" Erik cried. He ran toward the rubble. "Antoni!"

"Who's that?" Njall said, still grimacing from the taste of salt.

"One of Erik's friends we left behind in the ice castle," Frayka said.

"Are you sure?" Greeta said. "You're the last one who went inside. Were all of Erik's men still frozen there?"

Frayka nodded. "I tried making some of them move, but they couldn't. I managed to wrench Erik's head free. That's all."

Erik soon reached the rubble and disappeared into the tall grass surrounding it. "Antoni! Where are you?"

His lost friend called out a muffled answer.

Greeta led the others toward the hidden pile of rubble.

"We shouldn't go closer," Njall said. He pulled his dagger from where he kept it tucked under his belt. "It's probably a trap."

"Nonsense." Greeta turned to face him. "It's just Erik and Antoni."

"I doubt it," Frayka said. She withdrew her dagger. "Listen to me and Njall. No Northlander assumes there's no danger without proof!"

But before Greeta could answer, Erik emerged from the tall grass. He said, "You need to see this."

CHAPTER 3

Erik parted the tall beach grass to allow Greeta, Frayka, and Njall to pass.

Greeta walked to the foot of the pile of rubble that contained Antoni and studied it. Large chunks of black rocks made up most of the pile. Picking up a small rock the size of her fist, Greeta recognized its porous texture and light weight. "These are like the rocks in the Land of Ice."

"Exactly," Antoni's muffled voice said.

"Hang on," Erik said. "I'm coming back now." Erik climbed on top of the rubble and dug through it. With a grunt Erik hauled Antoni's head out of the pile. "We'll get you dug out and back to your normal self."

Antoni grinned. "Fancy meeting you here."

Njall stared in astonishment. "There's

more of those things?"

Erik glared at Njall. "Watch who you're calling a thing. We got feelings."

Njall turned to Frayka and Greeta. Pointing at Erik and Antoni's head, he said, "How many are there?"

Greeta looked up when Eric's sharp whistle pierced the air.

"Greeta, help us out!" Erik shouted, lobbing Antoni's head at her. "Catch!"

Instinctively, Greeta reached out and caught him.

"Thanks most kindly, my dear," Antoni's head said.

Holding Antoni's head in her hands made Greeta's skin prickle, but she reminded herself that she held only rocks, bits of wood, and moss that he'd used to create his head. After all, he'd once been alive like her.

Shuddering, Njall backed away from them.

"They're friends," Frayka told him.

Njall glared at her. "Friends?"

"Of sorts." Frayka crossed her arms. "They can help us."

Njall shuddered again, looking less than convinced.

Erik continued tossing more bits and pieces of Antoni toward Greeta. She nestled Antoni's head in the grass and gathered up everything that Erik threw.

"How did you get here?" she asked Antoni.

"Finehurst," Antoni said. Then he frowned. "But not Finehurst. I wager he used sorcery to leave some essence of himself behind. You did say you met him in your own country." Antoni paused and then corrected himself. He spoke to the others. "Here. We're in Greeta's home country now."

Greeta knelt beside him, arranging the bits of rubble into the shape of a body. "We're in the Great Turtle Lands, but we're also far south of my home. This is a place I've only heard of. It's as new to me as it is to you." She paused, realizing she wanted to know more. "But how did Finehurst do whatever he did?"

"I can't say for certain," Antoni said, watching her assemble his body parts of stone and wood. "We entered the ice castle with Erik and we stepped in the room that kept the dragon goddess bound and captured. A deep cold blasted us from all of the walls around us."

Frayka thudded next to Antoni's head. "That's what froze you in place?"

Antoni pivoted to look up at her. "Indeed. And we stayed frozen in place. When you came back and wrenched Erik's head free, you most likely saw that the rest of us couldn't move." Antoni's head shuddered. "It's hard to remember what I saw because it all happened so fast."

"Anything you can tell us will help," Greeta said.

Antoni said, "You left behind one final piece of the tapestry Finehurst used to bind Norah in her castle prison. I saw that tapestry strip slither out of the niche that once held Norah. At first I thought it was a snake until I recognized the cloth. Its threads separated. They multiplied and grew. It was Finehurst's magic."

Frayka snapped off a piece of beach grass and stuck one end in her mouth to chew. "How could that happen when Finehurst wasn't there?"

Opening his eyes, Antoni stared at Frayka. "I know little about sorcery, but I've heard of magic triggers. My great auntie used to tell stories of a powerful sorcerer who would set up magic traps. The sorcerer would find hiding places for the treasures he held most dear and then set up magic that would go into effect only if triggered by a would-be thief."

Greeta picked up more pieces and rearranged some parts of Antoni's new body. Looking up, she discovered a pleasant surprise: Njall had joined Erik in digging through the rubble. "You mean if someone went looking for his treasure?"

"Only when they got close to finding it," Antoni said. "Let's say Finehurst hid some treasure in the ice castle."

"Finehurst's treasure was Norah, the

dragon goddess," Frayka said.

"Precisely. The magic the sorcerer created would wait in hiding and do nothing to announce its presence. That way, no one would suspect any magic might be there. The magic is triggered only when someone gets close to finding the treasure."

"So why didn't it happen when we freed Norah?" Frayka said.

"I think I know," Greeta said. "Remember how she couldn't cross the moat? She became trapped at the castle."

"Clever," Antoni said. "That means even when you set the goddess free, she could not leave. I remember that moat of fire. When we first arrived at the ice castle, we disassembled our bodies and threw as much as we could of ourselves across the moat. We had no other way to cross it."

"And we had none at all," Frayka said pointedly. "You left us behind."

Antoni made a movement as though shrugging. "We had our own business to tend. We thought Finehurst lived at the ice castle and that we could coerce him into making us flesh and blood again." He glanced at Greeta. "We had no way of knowing Greeta knew him and that he'd left the Land of Ice long ago."

"But you still haven't answered my question," Greeta said. "If Finehurst wasn't there, why did we think we saw him?"

"It was the trigger magic," Antoni said. "Norah used you to get across the moat, which freed her from Finehurst's grasp. I believe that triggered what happened next. Just as I said, the tapestry strip you left behind snaked out and its threads came undone. But they arranged themselves into a pile that became level with our eyes. The threads shaped themselves into the image of a man."

"Finehurst," Greeta muttered.

"Precisely," Antoni said. "Finehurst."

"So that's what we saw," Frayka said, still chewing on her blade of beach grass. "It looked like Finehurst but it wasn't even a real man. Just something that looked exactly like him."

"And then the image of Finehurst raised its arms and caused the castle to explode. And us along with it. We were thrown into the castle ruins to form a ship. We swept high in the sky toward the east coast and landed on the shore."

Frayka groaned. "The sea is cold like ice at this time of year. If you put ice in the sea, it takes a long time to melt."

"Precisely, again," Antoni said. "Once we arrived here, the warm sea water began melting the parts of the ship made up of ice. The magical image of Finehurst picked up the ship and threw it inland." He sighed. "And the ship landed here. This pile of rubble that you see is what's left of it."

"And the image of Finehurst we followed," Greeta said. "What happened to it?"

"I wish I knew," Antoni said. "I've been buried here in this rubble."

Remembering the storm cloud that had pointed them to the path leading here, Greeta looked up to the skies again. A thin white cloud stretched above but it looked like nothing more than a simple cloud.

Norah is related to water, not the sky. She could use the storm cloud because it held rain, and it's most likely she manipulated the rain cloud to show us where to go.

Greeta stood and turned to look at the salt water river flowing nearby. Unlike any other river she'd seen, it ran inland instead of out to the sea.

A rattling sound made her turn back toward the pile of rubble that had recently been a ship.

Antoni rolled his head next to the bits of wood and rocks that Greeta had assembled into the shape of a body. The pieces snapped together as if magnetized, and his head connected to the small stones forming a neck. United with his new body, Antoni sat up and then stood. "I'd like to tell you how to find Finehurst's double or even Finehurst himself, but I'm afraid I've exhausted my usefulness," he said.

When the others walked away, another rattling sound stopped Greeta and made her look back at the rubble.

Black smoke seeped up through the rubble and hovered above it.

"Finehurst!" Greeta shouted. She pointed at the smoke and then turned toward her companions.

They halted and looked at her, but no one looked concerned.

"What about him?" Frayka called.

"He's here!" But when Greeta turned back toward the rubble, the smoke had vanished.

Is Finehurst toying with me?

Or trying to make me look unreliable?

"Of course he'd be here," Greeta said, fidgeting with excitement. "His ship crashed here after it left the beach. But just now the smoke came up out of the ground and ..."

Njall crossed his arms. "And what?"

Greeta looked everywhere and saw no trace of the black smoke. "I don't know. Maybe it flew away. Or sank back into the ground."

"That seems unlikely," Njall said. "There is no trace of smoke. Maybe you saw a shadow."

Without another word, Greeta's companions walked away.

Greeta ground her teeth, certain of what she'd witnessed moments ago.

CHAPTER 4

Greeta follow the others along the salt water river while they searched for the magical image of Finehurst.

While Erik and Antoni caught up with each other, the talk turned to the fact they now walked in a land unfamiliar to them and potentially dangerous. They grumbled and worried, each imagining a more horrific possibility than the next.

"You know what they say about the Land of Vines," Erik said.

"We call it the Great Turtle Lands," Greeta said. "Not the Land of Vines."

Ignoring her, Erik said, "We must be prepared for anything."

Antoni added, "It could all go wrong in a moment. We might be travelling our merry way now, but horrible natives might be throwing knives at our throats around the next bend."

"We could still go home," Njall offered helpfully. Seeming to lose his trepidation of Antoni, he now walked next to him and shared in the conversation.

Greeta motioned for Erik to join her by Frayka's side.

"There's no need to go back to the Land of Ice, and there's nothing to fear," Greeta said. "This land is my home. Its people are my people."

"But you said you've never been here before," Frayka said. "You said you've heard of this place." She hesitated. "What did you call it again?"

"The Land of Swamp Dragons," Greeta said.

"Wonderful," Frayka said. "Swamps and dragons."

"Don't forget the Vinelanders," Erik said. "They're deadly warriors, all of them. Horrible, screeching demons."

Antoni piped up. "And they'll slaughter us the moment they see us."

"Which is why we have to kill them first," Erik said. "On sight."

"No, we won't," Greeta said, struggling to keep her patience. "Back when we first met, I told you the story of how my Uncle Killing Crow saved my family when we arrived in the Great Turtle Lands."

"This would be the same uncle who meant to slaughter you on sight?" Erik said.

"Oh, I remember this story!" Frayka said, brightening. "He was getting ready to kill them when he saw Greeta shapeshift from a little dragon to a toddler girl." She winked at Erik. "And we all know Greeta can change into a dragon."

Everyone except Greeta laughed.

More than ever, she felt frustration at not having figured out how to control her ability to shapeshift. She didn't know anyone else who could do it and therefore had no one to teach her.

"Just because I don't know how to change into a dragon at will doesn't mean you shouldn't listen to me about not killing my people," Greeta said. "We believe in the principle of the seven generations: to consider how any decision will impact the next seven generations. And it doesn't matter whether that decision is large or small. It means putting yourself in the shoes of others and thinking about their feelings before you speak or take action."

The group became so silent that Greeta heard only their footsteps and the gentle flow of the river beside them.

Frayka broke the silence. "She's serious."

Everyone else exploded in laughter.

Frayka struggled to suppress a smile. "She looks like a Northlander, but she doesn't talk like one!"

"We are a peaceful people who value all life," Greeta said, hoping to reason with them. "We value life whether it's mortal, animal, or plant. All animals are our brothers and sisters."

Erik, his men, and Njall laughed longer and louder.

"Then why do we hear such terrifying stories about Vinelanders?" Frayka said. "Why do all Northlanders fear them so?"

"Striking terror into the hearts of our enemies is an act of peace," Greeta said. "If we can scare you away, then no one has to fight. No one has to die. And the next seven generations can live in peace and without threat of war."

"You have a lot to learn about being a Northlander," Frayka said.

Greeta pressed her lips together, willing herself to be quiet.

And you have much to learn about the Great Turtle Lands and its people.

CHAPTER 5

They trekked along the river for the rest of the day and set up camp alongside its banks that night. Greeta stared at the brilliant stars sparkling above until she fell asleep.

When she awoke in the familiar Northlands town of Guell, Greeta realized she hadn't come awake at all. Instead, she'd found her way into the Dreamtime, the mystical realm where Greeta could see the past and meet the dead.

The sun blazed high above instead of lower along the horizon, which meant she'd come to a different time of year in the Dreamtime. Looking out to the fields surrounding Guell, she saw its townspeople tending crops.

It's summer here, not winter.

A metallic hammering continued without stop. Greeta followed the sound to the smithery in the village center where she found her mother Astrid at the anvil. Greeta positioned herself a few steps away from the anvil until her mother stopped hammering and shoved the short length of metal she worked into a quenching barrel of water. Soot covered her face and hands. Even from a distance, her skin smelled like smoke.

"It's a dagger blade," Astrid said, looking into the water. "I remember ruining one several years ago because I let my emotions get the best of me. The iron wasn't holding heat the way I expected, and I got mad at it." She laughed and pulled the newly forged dagger blade out of the quenching barrel. Placing the blade on a bench, she turned toward Greeta and laughed. "That doesn't happen anymore."

Her mother's words bewildered Greeta, even though she suspected they held important information she needed. "I don't understand," Greeta said.

"You don't know how to control turning into a dragon, and that haunts you," Astrid said. "That's because you don't know enough about blacksmithing."

Greeta stared at her mother, feeling more bewildered than ever.

"Come with me," Astrid said, gesturing for Greeta to follow her inside the smithery. "It begins with finding a lump of iron in the ground. There used to be Boglands in the highest reaches of the Northlands. People would search through them to find chunks of raw iron. Then the Boglanders would smelt them." Astrid picked out a lump of iron from a barrelful. She held it in the palm of her hand. "The result is a bloom of iron like this, ready to smite."

Although tempted to complain that she couldn't see how a bloom of iron had anything to do with turning into a dragon, Greeta kept quiet and listened.

Astrid tossed the bloom back into the barrel. Taking Greeta by the hand, Astrid led her to the anvil. Letting go of Greeta's hand, Astrid picked a gray flake the size of a fingernail from the anvil's surface. "This is slag. It's a type of weakness inside iron. When you hammer iron, you force its weakness to come out, and this is what it looks like." She placed the piece of slag in Greeta's hand.

Strangely soft, it crumbled apart when Greeta touched it.

"Iron is like people," Astrid said. "Every piece of iron is unique, and every piece of iron has its own character. Some iron has great strength of character, and some iron is very weak in character. People are like iron."

"And you find out what kind of character the iron has when you hammer it?" Greeta hesitated. She had talked about this with someone before. Perhaps with Papa when he showed her how to make a dragonslayer's sword when they were in the Land of Ice? "No, that's not right. You can't tell the true character of any piece of iron until after you've forged it and someone uses it. If the iron's character is weak, it's likely to bend or break, which is terrible if you've made a sword. If its character is strong, the iron is flexible and strong instead."

Astrid smiled at her daughter. "Your father taught you well."

"But what about slag? If you can hammer out the weakness from iron, why doesn't that make all iron strong?"

Astrid sat down on the bench where she'd placed the newly made dagger and gestured for Greeta to sit next to her. Picking up the dagger blade, Astrid studied it and said, "Every mortal in your world has strengths and weaknesses. It's the mortal condition: no one can be entirely weak or entirely strong." Looking at Greeta, Astrid said, "We all have our weak points, no matter how hard we work to be strong. We can become stronger but mortals always have flaws. Iron is the same."

Greeta mulled over her mother's words. "Does that mean no matter how much you hammer any piece of iron that it still has weakness inside?"

"Yes. That's how we're like iron. But

we're different because we have the power to change."

"But that's the problem." Greeta felt frustration rising inside like stormy ocean waves. "I changed into a dragon one time. I don't know how it happened. I don't know how I changed back. I don't know how to control it."

Astrid nodded. "Northlander children were kept hidden away for that reason. When you're young you don't know how to control your own body or how to keep from changing others."

"Others?" Greeta's frustration shifted to confusion. "Northlanders could turn other people into dragons?"

Astrid laughed. "No. Nobody could change into a dragon. Northlanders could only change their mortal bodies slightly: they could become taller or shorter, heavier or thinner, stronger or weaker. I could bulk up my muscles to make my black-smithing work easier. The jeweler in our village made his fingers narrow and thin like tools to make his work easier. And we all did it by imagining how we wanted to look."

Her mother's words jogged Greeta's memory. "Papa told me something like that months ago when we sailed from home to the Land of Ice. But he said it was because you ate dragon meat."

"The blood of a dragon is what holds the

power," Astrid agreed. "Eating meat makes it possible to change shape because of the blood held inside the meat."

"I don't understand," Greeta said. "Papa says it's eating the meat that makes you change, but you said it comes from imagining things. Which one is true?"

"Both." Dagger still in hand, Astrid sat on the dirt floor of the smithery and carved drawings into it. First, she carved the images of two dragons. "There are two types of dragons: one is an animal and the other is a god that can appear as a dragon."

"Yes," Greeta said, drawing upon another memory. "Papa and Auntie Peppa told me about that."

Astrid drew a box around one dragon. "We respect the gods. We'd never harm them." She stabbed the center of the other dragon image. "But we kill the dragons that are animals. If we don't, they will kill us. And when we kill them, people eat dragon meat." Astrid paused, seeming to mull over her thoughts. "I believe everyone has the power to become a shapeshifter, but that power is hidden behind a locked door inside them. Most people don't even know they have it. I think the dragon blood inside the meat is like a key that unlocks a door. As soon as people eat dragon meat, they can shift."

Greeta sank to the ground and sat next

to her mother. "You said it's the blood, not the meat. Why?"

"Dragonslayers drink the blood, and it makes them stronger."

Greeta wished she hadn't asked.

Astrid dragged the point of her dagger from the dragon image she'd stabbed to draw an arrow toward a clear spot of dirt. She then drew a stick figure in the dirt. "If a dragon bites someone, that person dies in a few days because of the poison in the dragon's spit. And there is no cure for a dragon bite."

That fact made Greeta shudder.

"But eating dragon meat unlocks the door that makes it possible for what you think to transform the way you look and the way anyone you think about looks. The strength or weakness you see inside yourself becomes visible to others. And if you focus your attention on the strength or weakness you see in someone, then everyone else can see what you think of that person."

Mulling over her mother's words, Greeta said, "Then however I see myself will change the way I look and however I see somebody else will change the way they look?"

"Exactly," Astrid said. "And that's why Guell and all other Northlander villages had an unwritten law: You always have the right to change yourself, but you don't have the right to change others."

Greeta thought about her experience changing into a dragon months ago. "I don't remember thinking of myself differently when I turned into a dragon. I certainly didn't imagine myself as one." She paused, rethinking what they'd talked about so far. "But you said people can only change the way their mortal bodies look. They can't change into animals."

Astrid shrugged. "Usually not. There are rumors of people turning into deer when they meet a dragon because their fear turns them into animals. And one time I saw men turn into fish during a battle. I think they were scared, and that might be what turned them."

"I don't remember being scared," Greeta said. "I remember being angry."

"And have you ever caused anyone else's appearance to change or just your own?"

Greeta answered without hesitation. "Just my own."

Astrid sat up straight and held the dagger blade so that the light revealed the blade's pattern, which looked like dragon scales. "I don't think you're like other shapeshifters. You have turned into a dragon only once, and it wasn't fear that turned you."

"So what is it that lets me turn into a dragon? I don't think it was anger because

I've been angry plenty of times after that and stayed mortal. And I wasn't angry when I turned from a dragon into a woman. If it's not fear or anger, what is it?"

"I suspect two things," Astrid said. "First, I believe the dragon blood that runs in your veins is stronger than mine."

"So I am *part* dragon," Greeta said.

Astrid gave her a bemused smile. "Your father already admitted as much along with other things he probably shouldn't have revealed. But yes. You are part dragon."

"And the second thing?"

Astrid tilted the dagger blade, focusing her attention on its pattern. "I never knew I had changed into a dragon until after I died. I thought I'd had a dream about being a dragon, and it never dawned on me that it had been real."

Suddenly nervous, Greeta twisted her hands together. "What are you saying?"

"I never knew how to shift my shape into that of a dragon or shift back to myself." Astrid sighed. "I don't know how you can do that. It's something you're going to have to figure out for yourself."

Greeta nodded, realizing she'd suspected as much to be true. She covered her face with her hands and rubbed her eyes, letting her mother's words sink in. But when Greeta let her hands fall away and opened her eyes, she discovered Astrid and the village of Guell had vanished. Greeta found herself on the beach where she had landed days ago with Frayka, Njall, and Erik.

A woman walked out of the ocean. With the rising sun behind her, she appeared as a silhouette.

Greeta squinted and shaded her eyes with her hand. "Frayka?"

The woman strolled toward Greeta, tilting her head to one side. "Greeta?"

Squinting harder, Greeta struggled to figure out who she saw. The voice she heard didn't belong to Frayka, but Greeta recognized it nonetheless.

As if in spirit of cooperation, the sun ducked behind cloud cover.

Astonished, Greeta stared at the shaman she'd met in her home village months ago.

"There you are!" Shadow said. "I've been looking for you."

With a start, Greeta awoke.

Surrounded by her sleeping companions on the bank of the river, she saw no sign of Shadow.

CHAPTER 6

Still getting her bearings after waking up, Greeta became aware that her skin felt different. It seemed like a blanket wrapped too tightly. Groggy, she sat up, aware of chirping birds and the sound of the surrounding high grass rustling in the wind. The air had a faint fishy odor.

Greeta stretched her hands and winced at the tightness of her skin, which had turned red and ached with tenderness.

Njall groaned on Frayka's other side. "Why does my skin hurt?"

"Hey," Frayka said, sitting up next to her. "You and Greeta are sunburned."

Squinting at the sky above, Greeta said, "I don't understand. It's winter. The sun is too weak at this time of year to burn skin."

Njall sat up, staring at his hands. Swearing, he hiked to the nearby river and plunged his burned hands into the cold water, sighing with relief.

"You said your home is far north of here," Frayka said.

Annoyed at her own oversight, Greeta sank her face into her palms only to wince and cry out in pain.

"Your face is sunburned, too," Frayka said.

"It's because we're in the Land of Swamp Dragons," Greeta said. "Now I remember hearing stories about how the sun is much stronger here. That must be why it burned us." Glancing at Frayka, she said, "Although you don't look bad. You're barely pink."

"It'll fade to brown," Frayka said. "Thanks to my great-grandmother, my skin comes from the Far East."

Greeta envied Frayka her brown skin, not only because it weathered better in sunlight but because Greeta wished she could fit in among the dark-skinned people of her home, the Shining Star Nation.

Moments later, Greeta hiked up her pants legs and joined Njall standing waist-high in the river. Following his lead, she cupped cool water in her hands and sank her face into it, grateful for the relief it provided.

A large silver fish jumped out of the water and flew through the air between them.

"Breakfast!" Njall cried. Hampered by

the pressure of the rushing water surrounding him, Njall worked his way back
to the bank and then ran alongside it,
keeping up with the leaping fish.

Thinking she could help, Greeta followed. To the rest of her companions she called out, "We're fishing!"

Running after Njall, Greeta wondered
how he planned to catch it. In her Shining
Star village, her neighbors used nets to
fish. She knew Northlanders also caught
fish, but she hadn't been in Frayka's settlement long enough to learn how they did
it.

While following Njall, she looked for
anything they could use to scoop it out of
the river. Although Greeta practiced the
belief that all animals (including fish) were
her brothers and sisters, she also realized
most creatures ate other creatures. What
mattered was honoring and thanking the
fish for giving its life so that others could
live.

They followed the river as it wound
around a bend and down a slope. Up a-
head, the river forked in two directions:
the left branch ran into thick vegetation,
and the right side crossed an open field
where scraggly trees grew on the banks.
Leafless, the white-barked trees had short,
thick trunks and long, thin branches.

They reminded her of the gossiping
trees around the lake that she and Frayka

had slogged through in the Land of Ice. Greeta shook off that thought. The gossiping trees had done them no harm other than to spread the news of their existence.

The scales of a leaping fish gleamed in the sunlight. The fish plunged into the tumbling water at the river's fork.

Greeta caught up with Njall, who now stood on the bank's edge, waiting to see which direction the fish would take. She pointed at the water. "Look at how the water bubbles and churns. That means there's a bed of boulders beneath it. Maybe the fish got caught in the rocks."

Njall shook his head. "Fish are too slippery. It's hiding. It knows we want to catch it."

Greeta studied the river. "The stream on the left is tamer but looks deep. The fish might be hiding there. Or deciding which way to go. The branch on the right runs rough at the fork but then looks shallow."

The fish reappeared, leaping high in the air at the fork and then plopping into the water that forked to the right.

"Stay back!" Njall said. He raced ahead. Shouting distance away, he stepped into the shallow water, hands extended and ready to catch the fish. "Chase it toward me!"

The wind stirred, making the branches of the trees lining the river creak and groan.

Greeta saw a stick on the ground and picked it up. Taking time to be sure of her footing, she stepped into the water where the fish had last appeared. She felt silt and the smooth and round surface of small stones beneath her feet. She shifted her feet away from the stones and onto the silt of the riverbed. She looked into the water, now murky with clouds of silt from her movement. Greeta shifted her gaze ahead and caught a glimpse of something silver and quick. "It's heading your way!" she called to Njall.

Greeta kept her focus on stepping forward, careful with her steps and aware how the flowing water chilled her ankles. She also kept her stick in the water, ready in case the fish changed its course and came back toward her.

And then Njall screamed.

Greeta looked up, struggling to understand what she saw up ahead.

Black smoke rolled across the surface of the river and surrounded Njall. Squeezing him, the smoke took the shape of a dragon and lifted him up into the air.

The black smoke! It's Finehurst!

The smoke dragon deposited Njall in the branches of a tree.

Spiraling up into the air, the smoke dragon flew into the jungle.

Njall now hovered several feet above the river in the tree's grasp, water dripping from his feet.

Below, the fish jumped high enough to graze the soles of his feet before falling back into the water.

"Greeta!" Njall hollered. "Help me!"

A black vertical line gaped open in the trunk of the tree. Its branches moved Njall toward that gap.

Njall screamed again.

Greeta stared in disbelief while the branches of the tree stuffed a struggling Njall into the widening gap. Every time Njall succeeded in getting a handhold or foothold to gain purchase, the branches whipped his skin, drawing blood and forcing him to let go. Within seconds, the branches forced him inside the trunk and the black vertical slit sealed itself shut like a satisfied mouth.

The tree trunk bulged like a snake that had just eaten a rat.

Greeta scrambled back onto the bank of the river, ready to charge ahead.

But when she reached for her sword, Greeta realized she'd left it behind, lying on the ground where she'd slept.

CHAPTER 7

Greeta spun toward camp and yelled, "Frayka! Bring my sword!" She then bolted toward the tree trunk that had swallowed Njall whole and sank her fingers into the vertical slit that now pressed shut like lips determined to keep a secret.

"I don't have my sword!" Greeta yelled, hoping Njall could hear her.

Thick black sap lined the slit, and Greeta grimaced at the way it stuck to her skin and nails. When she tried to pry the slit open, it refused to budge. Instead, loose bark crumbled underneath her hands.

"Frayka!" Greeta cried again.

The leafless tree shifted and groaned. The branches towering above leaned down as if to get a better look at Greeta. Before she realized what was happening, a branch wrapped its flexible tendrils a-

49

round Greeta's waist and hurled her across the river where she landed on the opposite bank. The trees surrounding her on that bank turned to her with interest.

"Njall, I have to go back and get my sword!"

Before she could be devoured, Greeta sprinted toward the fork in the river where no tree could reach her. In the distance she saw Frayka appear over the top of the hill, followed by Erik and Antoni. Waving her arms above her head, Greeta cried out, "Here!"

While the others ran toward her, Greeta found a pathway through the river on the boulders sunk into its bed. She reached the other bank as they ran up to it.

Frayka carried Greeta's scabbard and sword in one hand and tossed them to her. "Where's Njall?"

Greeta strapped on the scabbard and withdrew her sword. "A tree ate him."

Erik and Antoni laughed.

Ignoring them, Greeta said, "We have to get him out."

Frayka pulled the dagger out from under her belt. "Which tree?"

Erik slapped Frayka on the back. "Greeta's pulling a trick on you. Trees can be wicked gossips, but they don't eat people."

Antoni giggled. "Everybody knows that."

Focusing on Frayka, Greeta pointed at the culprit. "It's the tree that looks like it's just eaten someone." After taking a few steps toward the tree, Greeta hesitated and turned back to face her companions. "Be careful. I think they're all hungry."

Erik and Antoni doubled over in laughter, while Frayka joined Greeta's side.

Approaching the tree, Greeta pointed at its bulging trunk. "That's Njall. I tried making its mouth open up, but it wouldn't budge. I think we should cut him out, but it's going to be tricky."

The tree swept a branch toward the women, but Greeta pushed Frayka back to keep them both out of reach.

Walking past them, Erik and Antoni howled with laughter. "Afraid of a little branch blowing in the wind?" Erik said.

Greeta said, "There's no wind right now."

"No wind." Erik pranced like a pony. "There's no wind."

Frayka said, "Let them find out the hard way."

The dead men sauntered among the trees lining the river until each one found himself snapped up in the branches of a tree with a gaping mouth.

They screamed.

Ignoring the dead men, Greeta and Frayka dashed toward the tree that consumed Njall.

"Protect me," Frayka said, now face-to-face with the vertical slit sealed shut with black sap. She struck it repeatedly with her dagger.

Nodding her agreement, Greeta gripped her sword with both hands and kept her back to Frayka. Casting a quick glance all around, Greeta saw no sign of Erik or Antoni. When a branch tried to grab Frayka, Greeta cleaved it in half with an overhead blow.

The tree cried out with its vertical mouth and revealed a glimpse of Njall inside.

When the mouth closed, Greeta heard Frayka say, "The trunk is too thick. I can't carve him out!" Nonetheless, Frayka kept attacking the tree with her dagger.

Greeta stayed on her toes, glancing from side to side. A branch grasped her head from above. Remembering her training with Margreet in the Dreamtime, Greeta swept her hands and sword back around the top of her head. She felt the force of the cut reverberate through the blade to the hilt in her hands. Tiny branches grabbed onto her hair, and the rest of the branch she'd severed fell to the ground at her feet.

The sensation made her feel as if spiders were crawling through her hair. Shuddering in revulsion, Greeta let go of her sword with one hand and ripped the tiny branches from her head.

She thought she heard the tree laugh.

"Greeta, look!" Frayka said. "This tree is ticklish."

Daring a quick glance over her shoulder, Greeta saw Frayka dragging the tip of her dagger blade across a groove in the bark. The tree shuddered. Its vertical slit of a mouth opened, air rushed out, and the sound of its exhale felt light and breezy.

Greeta turned back in time to slash at another menacing branch, but this one evaded her blow.

Keeping her back to Frayka, Greeta heard more scraping sounds and knew it had to be Frayka's blade dragging against the bark.

All above and around Greeta, the naked tree branches swooped and trembled. Finally, she felt a blast of air against her back.

"Greeta, help!" Frayka called out.

Greeta turned to see the tree's mouth gaping wide open and Frayka reaching in with one hand to clutch Njall. With the other hand, she kept tickling the tree with her dagger blade.

Sheathing her sword, Greeta wedged next to Frayka and reached into the tree trunk with both hands. She found Njall's leg and wrapped her hands around his knee and ankle. "Pull!" Greeta said.

Working together, the women hauled Njall out of the tree trunk. Covered in black sap, Njall shrieked and stumbled a-way from the tree line.

Frayka gave the bark one more satisfy-ing scrape with her blade, and the tree trembled with delight. "There," she told the tree. "See how unnecessary it is to eat my friends?"

Following Njall, Greeta and Frayka ran away from the tree line, barely escaping the desperate grasp of the tree that had swallowed him.

Dagger still in hand, Frayka stabbed it in the air at the trees. "And those others your friends ate? The trick is on you. They're already dead!" Taking a defiant step forward, Frayka slashed again at the air with her dagger. "Even worse, they aren't mortal! They're made of stone and plant and wood. Wood like you! You've eaten your own kind!"

The trees that had consumed Erik and Antoni shook with violent convulsions. Their narrow mouths opened and they spit the dead men out into the river. The trees pressed their mouths shut, but long trails of black-sap spit ran down their trunks, collecting between their exposed roots on the ground surrounding them.

CHAPTER 8

"Those wretched things almost killed me," Njall said. He groaned and sank into the grass.

He yelled at the trees, "That's what you get for trying to kill a Northlander! You're lucky we don't have time to chop you into firewood!"

Njall shivered briefly. Covered from head to toe with black sap, he extended his arms and stared at them in disgust. "This is horrible. I'll stick to everything I touch."

Greeta wiped her sap-covered hands against each other, but only managed to spread more of it across her skin.

Erik and Antoni walked toward her, their appearance darkened by the sap. Their stone bits had deepened in color, and the sap stained all of their wooden parts. With every step they took, water from their immersion in the river rolled off. "Thank you ever so much for your kind assistance in rescuing us from those cannibals," Erik said.

Greeta offered a sweet smile. "Perhaps next time you'll listen instead of laughing at us." Her hands stuck together for a moment and she struggled to separate them. "Besides, Frayka *did* help you. Didn't you hear her mocking those trees?"

"He can't hear much of anything," Antoni said. "Too much sap in his ears." Antoni leaned to the side and tapped his head. When nothing happened, he sighed and gave up. "In mine, too."

"All right," Erik said. He turned his back on Greeta. "Then I will tell Frayka, my *friend,* that she can scrub that sap off easier in water."

Anxious to try it, Greeta dashed into the river, sank her hands into the cool water, and rubbed them together. Within minutes, the black sap dissolved and washed away. Pulling her hands out of the water, Greeta sensed the softness and smoothness of her skin where the sap had covered it. Looking more closely, she saw the sap stained her skin in the same way it stained Erik and Antoni.

Hope rushed through her. All of Greeta's life, her pale white skin saddened her because it made her different from her dark-skinned friends and community. Months ago she'd lost the man she thought to be the love of her life only to learn the truth when she overheard him ridiculing Greeta behind her back. She doubted any other man would ever want to marry her and expected to live her life alone.

Holding her stained hands up in the sun, Greeta smiled at the beauty of the parts of her skin that had browned very slightly. Then she noticed something else. She climbed out of the river and raced to tell Frayka and Njall what she discovered. "Look," she said, holding her hands out for them to see. "The tree sap healed my skin where the sun burned it. See how the pink color is gone? The tenderness is gone, too. My skin feels perfect now."

Njall still sat on the ground. Squinting at her, he said, "You look funny."

"Look, I'm the same color as Frayka now." Greeta held her colored hand next to Frayka. Even though the sap had darkened Greeta's skin, it still looked pale next to Frayka's skin. "Maybe I'm a little darker, but that's wonderful! I think this sap will protect us from getting too much sun."

Njall pointed at her. "But you're splotchy."

Greeta kneeled next to him. "You could help with that. Do you mind if I scrape off some of the sap from you so I can spread it all over my skin?"

Snorting, Njall laughed. "If you want to help me clean up, be my guest."

Beaming with delight, Greeta cupped her hands and ran them along Njall's arms and back to collect plenty of sap. She then rubbed it on her face and every bit of exposed skin. "Come on, Njall. Erik's right. It washes away easily once you get in the water."

"You go ahead," Njall said. "It might take time for me to pry loose from the ground."

Happily, Greeta ran back and plunged into the river. She ran her hands across her arms and face to smooth out her new color. Once satisfied, she emerged just as Njall made his way into the water.

Leaving Njall behind in the river, Greeta joined Frayka, who stood on the bank, deep in discussion with Erik and Antoni.

"Do you think those trees are natural or enchanted?" Frayka said.

"The man-eating trees?" Greeta said in surprise. "They must be enchanted?"

"Not necessarily," Antoni said. "There can be some mighty peculiar things in nature."

"Like dragons," Erik said. "And shape-shifters."

Greeta shrugged. "What does it matter whether they're part of nature or enchanted?"

"Because we're deciding which fork of the river to follow," Frayka said. "If they're enchanted, it might be Finehurst's doing. It might be his way of scaring us away from his path. But if they're a freak of nature, then we should consider the other fork of the river."

"Never mind that," Greeta said. "I saw the smoke again, and this time it took the shape of a dragon."

Erik and Frayka exchanged worried glances.

"A dragon," Frayka said in disbelief. "Made of smoke."

"If you don't believe me, ask Njall. The smoke dragon picked him up off the ground and put him in the branches of the tree that ate him."

Turning toward the river, Frayka shouted, "Njall! Greeta says you saw a smoke dragon."

Shouting back, Njall said, "It's the thing that threw me to the trees!"

Greeta smiled sweetly at Frayka's and the dead men's surprise. "Finehurst is trying to kill us," Greeta said. "Or make himself enough of a threat to keep us from following him."

"What do you suggest?" Erik said.

Greeta pointed in the direction where she'd last seen the smoke dragon. "That's where Finehurst headed. That's where we need to go."

CHAPTER 9

Greeta led Frayka, Njall, and the two dead men into a terrain unlike anything they'd seen before. Trees that neither gossiped nor tried to eat them spread far and wide. Their bark appeared thick and brittle. Thin branches arced high and swept down to the spongy ground, thick with moss. The forest canopy held in heat and moisture, leaving the air dense with humidity and thrumming with the sound of insects.

Njall walked between Frayka and Greeta. Ignoring Greeta, Njall looked at Frayka and said, "I thank you for saving my life."

Frayka shrugged. "Wasn't just me. Greeta did most of the work."

"No!" Njall protested. "I could hear everything when that horrible thing tried to digest me. I know you're the one who figured out how to get its wretched mouth open." Njall's voice softened. "I never realized how clever you are."

Njall's presence forced Greeta closer to the declining slope of the river bank. Noting how easily she could slip and fall, Greeta opted to weave in front of him. Looking over her shoulder she said, "You certainly didn't realize her cleverness when you called her Frayka the Freak."

He waved his hand in front of his face to shoo away annoying gnats. "That happened a very long time ago."

Frayka laughed. "It happened months ago when the ice dragons caused the ground to split apart around the settlement."

"And that was a very long time ago," Njall said, sidling up close to Frayka. "That day I saw your courage when you faced the ice dragons alone and fought them."

Greeta spun to face him, walking backwards while she talked. "I fought the ice dragons, too. Frayka killed one, I killed another, and the last one got away."

Ignoring her, Njall kept his focus on Frayka. "And now today you risk your own life to save mine."

"Anyone would have done it," Frayka said. "And like I said, Greeta did the most to haul you out of that tree." She winked at Greeta. "Except I'm not convinced she'd be willing to do it again until you acknowledge what she did for you."

Njall gave Greeta a quick glance. "I appreciate the way you helped Frayka save my life."

Greeta turned her back on him to face forward while she walked. Smiling, she remembered how she'd wondered about Frayka's claim to see the future in the portents she experienced, especially because she'd insisted Njall must become the father of her children.

Frayka still seemed to tolerate Njall's presence rather than love him. But Frayka had made it clear love had nothing to do with it: her portents had shown her that only Njall could make it possible for Frayka's children to inherit her ability to portend the future. And Frayka believed the safety and very existence of her people depended on that ability.

The river slowed and widened to end in a massive swamp.

Erik and Antoni brushed past Greeta and hurried several steps ahead of her. They paused, scanning the water and soft mossy ground.

Catching up with them, Greeta said, "What's wrong?"

"There," Erik said, pointing back in the direction of Frayka and Njall. "See that ripple in the water?"

Greeta squinted, unable to detect it.

"Isn't that just the river current?"

"Since when does a current have a pair of beady eyes?" Antoni said.

Greeta kept looking until she saw a distinct ripple behind glistening eyes and a bony ridge above them. Pulling her sword out of the scabbard, she said, "Frayka, Njall, look! There's something in the water!"

Turning to look, Frayka and Njall each drew their daggers and stared at the ripling water.

Greeta said, "Erik, what do you think that is?"

When Erik failed to answer, Greeta turned to discover that he and Antoni had vanished.

"They're gone!" Greeta shouted to Frayka and Njall. "Erik and Antoni. They're gone!"

"It's up to us, then," Frayka said. "It's not the first time they've deserted us."

A long scaly tail and ridged lizard body emerged from the water's surface. Its scales reflected the sunlight with a greenish-gray hue. Eyes rested in the sockets of a face with a long jaw filled with dozens of sharp teeth.

"It's a dragon," Greeta said. She adjusted her grip on the sword.

"There's another one!" Njall cried, pointing to where Erik and Antoni had stood moments ago. Its tail whipped back and forth in the water while it swam toward them.

"I've never seen dragons like these before," Greeta said. "A dagger might not kill them. Climb the trees. I'll handle this!"

"No!" Njall said. "I've had enough of trees for one day, thank you very much."

"Can dragons climb trees?" Frayka said.

"I don't know," Greeta said. "But go now before it's too late. I'll hold them back."

Everything Greeta had ever learned from the people in her Shining Star homeland came rushing to mind. Whenever an animal failed to recognize a mortal as its brother or sister, the best course of action was to stand tall and remind that animal. Typically, the animal would feel regret at its insensitivity toward the mortal and run away in shame.

Greeta held the sword out to one side and stood her ground. Facing the water, she shouted in the Shining Star language, "I am Greeta of the Shining Star nation. I arrive as your guest. I am your sister!"

The nearest dragon darted out of the water in a blinding flash. The underside of its body hung so low that it scraped the ground.

It startled Greeta so much that she took several steps back and stumbled over a pile of rocks.

"Run!" she called to Frayka and Njall. "One bite will kill you!"

The dragon charged Greeta and snapped at her feet before she could regain her balance.

"What is wrong with you?" she shouted at the dragon. "Don't you understand? I am your sister!"

The pile of rocks she'd stumbled across stood up and quickly assembled into Erik. The dead man leapt upon the dragon and slammed against its body. Erik took off his own stony head and pounded it against the startled face of the dragon until the animal backed away and slithered into the water.

Greeta scrambled to her feet in time to witness the other dragon pouncing upon Frayka.

There is something wrong with these animals! They won't listen to reason!

Anger washed through Greeta and the desire to protect herself and her friends overwhelmed her. Charging toward the animal, Greeta raised her sword and chopped it across the dragon's tail, hoping to distract the monster.

But instead of cleaving the dragon's tail in half, Greeta's sword bounced off its tough scales, leaving the creature unscathed.

The dragon skittered off of Frayka and charged Greeta. Panic rushed through her, but she held on tight to the sword's grip and let the training she'd performed with Margreet take over. Greeta slashed the sword diagonally in front of her several times to distract the dragon while she took several long steps back in order to distance herself from it.

Another pile of rocks assembled itself into Antoni, who pounced on the dragon.

Whipping its tail wildly, the dragon wrenched itself toward Antoni's attack. The animal clawed at the air as if uncertain what had happened. All the while, Antoni hit the animal repeatedly with his rocky hands.

Gathering himself once more, Erik joined in the attack.

Greeta circled them and adjusted her hands on the grip. Margreet had taught her how to defend herself against people, not dragons. Her hands still stung from the way the sword had bounced off the scales. But watching it twist and turn under the dead men's blows, Greeta saw the dragon's soft and unprotected throat. "Flip it over!" she cried. "On its back!"

Erik and Antoni wrestled with the dragon and its snapping jaws.

Greeta gave in to the rawness of her emotion instead of the calm reasoning she'd learned from the Shining Star nation. She crept closer to the dead men and the dragon they now pinned to the ground. She held the grip high with the blade pointing toward the ground. All she needed was one clear shot at the dragon's throat in order to drive the sword point into it.

But while the dead men struggled with the dragon, Greeta felt something rush past her like a harsh wind.

"No!" Frayka cried out. "Stay away, Njall!"

Turning toward her, Greeta saw the other dragon clamp its jaws around Frayka's leg while Njall grabbed the animal's tail and pulled. Letting go of Frayka's bleeding leg, the dragon lunged toward Njall and clamped its teeth on his arm.

The damage had been done.

Greeta remembered what her mother told her in the Dreamtime about dragon bites.

There is no cure.

Frayka and Njall would be dead within the next few days.

CHAPTER 10

Before Greeta could take a step, the sound of an unfamiliar voice stopped her.

"Chaca!" a woman's voice called. "Zolten!"

The words sounded strange to Greeta's ears but seemed like names.

The dragon clenching Njall's arm immediately released it and skittered away.

The other dragon entangled with Erik and Antoni wriggled loose and also ran free.

Greeta gazed in astonishment at the sight of the two dragons running to nestle at the woman's feet.

Like all people of the Great Turtle Lands, the woman was petite, head and shoulders shorter than the Northlanders. The woman had painted her face white and decorated it with small brown dots.

The paint on her buckskin dress matched the pattern on her face.

But the most startling sight was her large headdress made of small white flowers and thick leafy vines. If the woman hadn't shouted, she would have blended in so perfectly among the trees that it would have been impossible to see her.

That realization reminded Greeta of a story Papa often told her about dragonslayers who did similar things to blend in with their surroundings while hunting dragons.

But this woman didn't appear to be a dragonslayer. If anything, the dragons acted as if they were members of her tribe.

Or her allies.

Hoping the woman might understand the language of the Shining Star nation, Greeta switched from speaking in Northlander to Shining Star. "Our people are hurt. Can you help us?" Greeta knew Frayka and Njall didn't have much longer to live, but she wanted however much time they had left to be comfortable.

The Swamp Lander woman stared at Greeta in blank confusion.

Looking back, Greeta saw Njall remove his shirt and tear it into strips. He used them to bandage Frayka's wound.

Facing the Swamp Lander woman again, Greeta said the few words from other languages that Uncle Killing Crow had helped her learn.

The Swamp Lander woman stopped her and repeated a few of the words Greeta spouted.

"Yes!" Greeta said in the Shining Star language, happy to see the woman respond.

When the Swamp Lander woman took several steps toward Greeta, the flower-and-leaf headdress rustled. The dragons walked at her heels. The Swamp Lander woman spoke rapidly while pointing at Frayka and Njall, but Greeta understood nothing she said.

When silence fell, Greeta pointed at herself and said, "Greeta." In turn, she pointed at Frayka and Njall and spoke their names.

Erik and Antoni gathered around the other Northlanders. "Waste no time," Erik said. "Kill her."

"No," Greeta said. "We don't know anything about her yet." Silently, she hoped the strange woman would help.

"Isn't it bad enough that you waited for those creatures to bite us?" Frayka said. Her face strained with anger. "We're going to die because you didn't kill them. This wasn't supposed to happen! You've ruined the portent about Njall!"

"Portent?" Njall gave Frayka a sharp look. "What portent?"

Frayka shouted at Greeta, "You've ruined everything!"

"I tried to chase them away," Greeta protested. "It's not my fault!"

"Give us the satisfaction of seeing our murderers destroyed." Njall finished wrapping Frayka's foot and now bandaged his own injured arm. "Kill her."

The Swamp Lander woman pressed her lips together. After a few long moments, she finally said, "Jaya."

Greeta didn't know if the woman was telling them her name or giving them a command. It had to be her name.

Jaya once again said, "Chaca! Zolten!" She pointed at Greeta and her companions.

The swamp dragons circled around the Northlanders until the animals stood behind them.

Greeta jumped when the creatures snapped at her.

Jaya gestured for the Northlanders to follow her.

"I think we're being captured," Greeta said. Looking at Frayka's bandaged foot, Greeta asked, "Can you walk?"

Frayka hobbled a few steps. "Of course, I can walk. But what are you waiting for? Use your sword, Greeta. Kill her and those wretched animals."

"You and Njall need help. If she's capturing us, maybe that means you'll get help." Greeta didn't want to dwell on the fact that her Northlander companions would soon be dead. "Let's go with her." She walked forward.

"No!" Frayka shouted. "She's the enemy!"

"You don't know what you're walking into," Erik said, still sitting on the ground. "How do you know you won't be walking into a den of dragons?"

Greeta strained to think, but her mind went numb.

Jaya crossed her arms and spoke again, this time slowly and with deliberation. Her firm and beleaguered tone told Greeta that she might be repeating what she had said moments ago, perhaps thinking that speaking more plainly might make them understand.

"We're in a land we don't know or understand," Greeta told her friends. "Frayka and Njall have mortal injuries. We should take the chance that being captured means we can get food and water." Greeta paused, distressed by the truth she faced. "And maybe a more comfortable place to die."

"How can you say these things? It makes more sense to kill that woman and her dragons than look for comfort." Frayka shook her head in dismay. "How did your Northlander blood get so damaged?"

"It's up to us," Njall told Frayka. "We will do what must be done." But when he tried to raise a threatening dagger, Njall grimaced in pain and hunched forward like an old man.

The swamp dragons edged closer and snapped at Njall's heels.

"We're going with Jaya," Greeta said. "Unless you'd rather get bitten again." Greeta glanced at Jaya and then walked ahead, hoping everyone else would follow and not attempt to murder anyone.

CHAPTER 11

The deeper they walked into the swamp, the thicker the air became. Sweat poured in rivulets down Greeta's face, chest, and back. She pulled at her clothes to keep them from sticking to her skin. A black insect landed on her knuckle, bit it, and then buzzed away before she could slap it.

"This is a terrible idea!" Frayka said while she walked next to Greeta. She pointed at Jaya, now walking ahead of them with the two swamp dragons close at her heels. "She's a monster!"

Greeta wondered why Frayka and Njall didn't act more concerned about their dragon bites and imminent death until she remembered all the stories Papa and Auntie Peppa told her about Northlanders. Greeta assumed those stories about fierceness in battle and the Northlander belief in a joyous life after death to be exaggerations, but now she believed them.

"Jaya isn't a monster," Greeta said, keeping her tone even and calm. "She is a native of the Great Turtle Lands. Like me."

"She is nothing like you." Frayka waved her hands to illustrate her words. "She wears plants on her head. And paints her face. And wears strange clothes."

Greeta willed herself to stay peaceful. "I imagine our clothes look just as strange to her. And that Jaya finds us just as peculiar as she seems to us."

"It's no reason to trust her." Frayka heaved a burdened sigh. "We should fight her to the death instead. These dragon bites will kill us soon. Why should we suffer when we could die in battle?"

"Frayka's right," Njall said, joining them. "As a Northlander, I commit to fearlessness in the face of certain death."

Greeta said, "Jaya belongs to the Land of Swamp Dragons, which is part of the Great Waters nation in the Great Turtle Lands. We come from different nations, but we come from the same land. We believe in the seven generations."

Njall's face screwed up in confusion. "What seven generations?"

"Don't ask," Frayka said, swatting at a few gnats hovering in front of her eyes.

"It's what all people who live in the Great Turtle Lands believe in," Greeta said, answering Njall's question. "Before any one of us makes a decision, we consider how that decision might affect the next seven generations of our people."

"That makes no sense." Njall scoffed. "You hunt or fish or trade to survive. You have a family to carry on your name and your blood. What's to consider?"

Frayka shifted a few steps to walk on the other side of Njall. "You're confusing Greeta with a Northlander. Just because she looks like us doesn't mean she's like us." Frayka gestured at Jaya, still leading the small group. "Greeta is more like her than us."

"You're suspicious of Jaya because you don't understand her," Greeta said. "And the worst thing we can do right now is be suspicious when she's helping us."

Frayka raised an eyebrow. "How can you believe she's helping us?"

"Because she's working with us, not against us." Greeta flinched when a dark memory crossed her thoughts. "The worst thing we can do is be disloyal to other women."

Frayka clapped her hands together in front of her face and then brushed the gnats she'd killed off her palms. "So that's what this is about."

"What?" Njall said. "You know something I don't?"

"Greeta's man betrayed her," Frayka

said. "Sounds like it was her cousin's fault: married, children, and would rather steal Greeta's man than be faithful to her own. Greeta blames them both, as she should."

Njall gave Greeta a pointed look. "We're not your cousin. Or your man."

Jaya stopped.

The others bumped into her.

Jaya tilted her head back, looking skyward. The vines and white flowers forming her headdress fell away from her shoulders and looked like a waterfall of foliage tumbling from the top of her head.

A dark cloud hovered high above.

Jaya called out to it and then waited patiently.

Minutes later, the cloud rumbled. Sparks of yellow light ignited inside the cloud and illuminated it like fireflies on a moonless night.

Jaya spoke again. This time her voice rose as if asking a question.

The cloud rumbled immediately as if in response.

Jaya spun to face everyone standing behind her. Gesturing toward Erik and Antoni, who lingered far behind the others, Jaya called out.

The two dragons skittered toward the dead men at an alarmingly fast pace, reaching them in seconds.

"What's the problem?" Erik cried, standing still while the dragons circled him.

"I don't know," Greeta said. "I can't understand Jaya or anything she's doing."

One of the dragons sniffed at Antoni and then gnawed on his stony foot after ripping it free from his body. "Not to worry!" Antoni shouted. "Plenty of other good stones around here I can use to replace it. No harm done."

Greeta struggled to keep her composure. "Stay calm, everyone."

The other dragon snapped at Erik.

"Here now!" Erik said, his voice strained and offended. "What did I ever do to you?" Crossing his arms in defiance, Erik snorted, "Filthy beast!"

Jaya called out to the dragons.

Simultaneously, they lifted their heads and turned to look at her.

She spoke, gesturing toward the Northlanders this time.

The dragons trotted away from the dead men and toward the mortals, but one animal kept Antoni's foot inside its mouth and gnawed on it. Each dragon nosed Njall and Frayka briefly before turning to Jaya and waiting expectantly.

The Northlanders drew their daggers and aimed at the dragons.

"Don't," Greeta said. "Those daggers will slide right off their scales."

Frayka and Njall were drenched with sweat. They looked like it took all they could muster to stand.

The dragon bites are making them sick.

"Please," Greeta said.

After exchanging frustrated glances, the Northlanders tucked their daggers away.

Instead of speaking, Jaya nodded toward Greeta.

The dragon carrying Antoni's stone foot in its teeth charged toward Greeta and then hauled itself up on its squat hind legs. In another few steps it stood face-to-face with Greeta and placed its muddy front paws on her shoulders.

Greeta struggled to stand still with its heavy weight leaning against her. She flinched and turned her face away from its teeth and foul breath. Her heart raced so quickly that Greeta felt her blood rushing through her body. She wanted to run away but knew she had to convince herself to stay put.

Don't panic. It might bite if it feels startled.

Thin and transparent eyelids blinked over its beady amber eyes. The creature stared into Greeta's eyes, its expression frighteningly intelligent and purposeful. Its jaw gaped open, filled with dozens of needle-like teeth. It then chewed on Antoni's foot.

Greeta turned her head away from its foul breath.

The creature moaned and leaned forward to rest its chin on Greeta's shoulder.

Although these dragons were far smaller and differently colored than the one she'd seen in Finehurst's possession near her Shining Star home, it reminded Greeta of what she'd felt when she'd seen her first dragon. Despite the shock and terror, she also felt a depth of kinship with it.

The dragon heaved a tremendous sigh, and some of the spit that covered Antoni's foot dripped onto Greeta's shoulder. Without ceremony or warning, the animal's paws slid off her shoulders, leaving muddy prints on Greeta's clothing. It padded back to Jaya's side, plopped to the ground, and chewed on Antoni's foot.

The remaining dragon opened its jaws and nudged its forehead against Greeta's shin. It slithered between her legs. The dragon brushed so hard against one leg that Greeta struggled to keep her balance. It looked up at Greeta, seeming to study her. Appearing to be satisfied, the dragon scampered back to Jaya and licked her foot. Jaya cocked her head to one side and stared at Greeta.

"What was that?" Frayka said. She hobbled next to Greeta. "Why didn't they bite you the way they bit us?"

"Perhaps," Njall said in an ironic tone, "these dragons recognize us as true Northlanders who won't hesitate to kill them. And they know Greeta won't hurt them because she's not a true Northlander."

Unable to look at her companions, Greeta said, "I don't know why they left me alone."

But she suspected the swamp dragons had detected the part of Greeta that made it possible for her to transform and be like them.

Is it only the swamp dragons that recognize what I can do?

She wondered if Jaya suspected Greeta had the ability to turn into a dragon.

CHAPTER 12

For the rest of the day they followed Jaya and her dragons through the swamp. The heat and humidity persisted, worse than ever. Insects filled the canopy of trees with their ear-piercing and vibrating songs. Thick veils of moss hung from the branches. The spongy ground narrowed to a thin trail surrounded by stagnant water covered by a bright green film.

By the time the setting sun turned wisps of clouds pink, the swamp gave way to a forest. The air surrounding them became more comfortable.

The forest gave way to a field. The spongy ground led to dirt so dry that every step raised a cloud of dust. Wilted grass indicated a lack of rain. In the distance, a deep-throated animal made hooting noises.

After following Jaya around a sharp bend in the trail, the sight of square stone pillars marking the edge of the forest surprised Greeta. The color of sand, each pillar towered as high as the surrounding trees. Instead of the roundness of trunks, the pillars' edges were clean and sharp. Even more impressive, peculiar symbols and images had been carved within hand-size square frames organized into rows and columns on the surfaces of the pillars.

A closer look at the illustrated pillars and the carvings inside the square frames revealed profiles of people with large noses that reminded Greeta of beaks. Others were symbols like the painted dots on Jaya's face. Some even looked like animals.

A large man stood between the two pillars. He wore a headdress of naked branches. Yellow clay colored his buckskin pants and bare chest. White paint in the image of a skull covered his face, making his eyes look deep-set and as black as a bottomless pit. He held a large knife made of carved stone.

Jaya spoke to him, gesturing toward Greeta and her band of fellow travelers.

The large man standing between the pillars pointed at Greeta but spoke to Jaya, who nodded. He then stepped aside and gestured for the Northlanders to pass between the pillars.

But once Greeta, Frayka, and Njall

walked past the pillars and the dead men stepped forward, the Swamp Lander man shrieked and stood between the pillars with his knife raised.

Looking back, Greeta saw Erik and Antoni standing still while Jaya and the large man argued.

The swamp dragon chewing on Antoni's foot lumbered forward. Opening its jaw, the animal let the stone fall from its mouth and land on the ground in front of Antoni.

"That's an improvement," Erik said. "At least you've got your foot back. Maybe the dragon likes you more now that it's had a good taste of you."

Antoni sighed. "Or perhaps it simply grew tired of its plaything."

Standing firm, the large Swamp Lander man pointed behind the dead men and spoke what sounded like a firm command to them.

"Relegated to the swamps, it looks like," Njall said. "I suppose this is the last we'll see of Erik and Antoni."

Glancing at him, Greeta saw blood staining his bandage. Taking a look at Frayka's foot, Greeta saw her bandage bore a deeper stain.

"Not everyone can get along with the dead," Frayka said.

But Frayka and Njall will be dead soon. Will they come back to haunt me? Have we been exposed to enough of Finehurst's magic that they'll become like Erik and Antoni?

Greeta shook away those thoughts. They'd arrived at a place that promised some type of village must be nearby. Surely they'd soon find a place where Frayka and Njall could be comfortable in their last days.

"Fare well," Erik called out. He remained standing in front of the Swamp Lander man. When he spoke, sarcasm and disappointment laced his voice. "No need to worry about us. Or make any attempt whatsoever to help."

"We'll find out if Finehurst came here," Greeta said. "I'm sure we'll meet up in a few days. Maybe you should stay on the outskirts and wait for us."

Erik gave Greeta a dark glance before walking away with Antoni.

Greeta chose not to worry about him. Erik and Antoni seemed to forget the troubles of the living. Right now Greeta only cared about Frayka and Njall.

After they'd marched through the jungle for awhile, Njall turned to Frayka and said, "What portent did Greeta ruin? When the dragons bit us, you said Greeta ruined everything."

Anger strained Frayka's face once more. "I suppose it will do no harm to reveal it now that you and I will be dying soon."

She glared at Greeta. "The portent is that only one Northlander man can give me children who can also read portents. That man is you."

Njall glowed with joy but then glowered. "Greeta!"

Greeta ignored him.

"She's hopeless," Frayka said. "As are our people. Now they will have no one to read portents and protect them."

Following Jaya on a path that took another sharp turn through the trees, the sight around that bend astonished Greeta so much that she stopped in mid-step.

A sprawling city of wide-open plazas paved in white stone stood beyond the tree line.

Several enormous stone buildings, all painted crimson red, were scattered among the plazas. They made the city look as if it were spattered with the blood of gods.

A crimson flat-top pyramid made of giant stair steps dominated the center of the city, surrounded by dusty avenues filled with thousands of people and more voices than Greeta ever imagined could exist in one place.

Huge red stone towers with slanting roofs made of black clay tiles stood like sentinels at the four corners defining the boundaries of the city. Each storey of the tower was smaller than the one below it, creating a wrap-around balcony on each floor.

Nearby, rows of ten-foot high stone columns lined a marketplace where vendors placed their wares on wooden carts décorated with brightly colored cloth awnings. Exotic scents spiced the air.

Bright white stone covered the ground throughout the entire city. Hollow channels carved into the stone ran in all directions.

Beyond the plazas, vast stretches of crops surrounded the city. Thousands of tiny white stone huts with tall thatched roofs dotted the boundary between the farmland and the city. Greeta guessed they must be homes, each one looking like it could contain nothing more than a single square room.

Jaya led the Northlanders through the crowds.

Realizing Jaya and the others had outpaced her, Greeta ran to catch up.

The sea of people surrounding Greeta overwhelmed her. Their bodies pressed against hers, smelling of sweat. Their voices hovered in the air, droning like insects and making her ears go numb. Her ribs squeezed tight against her chest while Greeta struggled to breathe, thinking the air must be thin with so many other people breathing it.

Many of the residents wore little more

than a short skirt and bright blue, yellow, or red paint on their skin. Men and women alike wore large metal hoops in pierced ears and noses. Like the carvings Greeta had studied at the guarded gate to the city, many people had large noses that reminded her of beaks.

The Swamp Landers exhibited no fear of the two dragons trotting by Jaya's heels. The crowd gave them wide berth but offered the creatures little more than a passing glance.

The brilliant hues that colored the Swamp Landers' clothing and skin dazzled Greeta.

Wide-eyed and speechless, Greeta joined Frayka and Njall in gawking at the wonders surrounding them. She stared at each towering building they passed.

The wide open sky reminded her of walking the beach by her home village in the Shining Star nation.

Jaya took them to a far side of the city where the crowds thinned and onto a narrow path decorated with stones of many colors. The path led to a large square platform supporting a pale yellow stone building.

On each side of the platform, twenty wide but shallow steps allowed an easy climb. An open doorway bisected each outside wall of the building, as well as a window opening on each side of the doorway.

Two rows of black stones lined the highest reach of each wall. A square cap rose like a small tower perched on the middle of the building's flat roof.

Greeta's first impression of the building was that it reminded her of a face: window openings for eyes, doorway for a nose, and black stones for eyebrows.

After climbing the steps, Jaya's two dragons plopped on either side of the open doorway, basking in the sun on the hot gray rock surface of the platform. Jaya gestured for the Northlanders to enter.

Frayka cleared her throat. "Is this a good idea?"

"Jaya acts like she's helping us," Greeta said. "If Jaya meant us harm, she would have left you to die in the jungle. Of course it's a good idea."

Casting a dark glance at Greeta, Frayka said, "You trust too easily."

"And you're stingy with your trust," Greeta said. "You make people do far more than needed to earn it."

"But that's just the thing. Trust is something to be earned." Frayka looked at the building with trepidation. "Not something to be given lightly."

"Maybe that's true in the Northlands and the Land of Ice. But you don't know the people of the Great Turtle Lands," Greeta said. Determined to prove a point, she entered the building without hesitation. Once inside, she came to a sudden stop because the darkness inside blinded her. Despite its open doorways and small window openings, a heavy dimness filled the stone building, and Greeta held her breath while she waited for her vision to adjust.

"Greeta?" A familiar voice drifted through the darkness like a lost spirit.

Moments later Greeta felt Red Feather's arms wrapped around her and his head buried against her shoulder. She relaxed, happy to be reunited with the brother of the sweetheart who jilted her.

CHAPTER 13

"Do you know this little man?" Frayka said, following Greeta inside the stone building. "Or have we finally found people who are friendly by nature?"

Njall joined Frayka's side. "Look how tiny he is! Barely stands as high as her chest."

Startled by Red Feather's embrace, Greeta felt dumbfounded and let her arms hang by her side. Being held in his sure and strong arms made her heart race. At the same time, she felt unsure of her feelings toward him and confused at finding him so suddenly and unexpectedly.

Her lifelong loyalty and love for Red Feather's brother Wapiti tugged at her like quicksand. Greeta reminded herself that Wapiti had betrayed her.

Do I still love Wapiti? How can I after

what he did? Am I only trying to shift my love for Wapiti to a brother who resembles him?

Am I having these feelings because they're convenient or because they're real?

Red Feather released her and stepped back before she could touch him. He spoke rapidly, his voice filled with relief. "Shadow promised we'd find you, but I'd given up hope."

Jaya interrupted and spoke to Red Feather while pointing at Frayka's and Njall's bandaged wounds.

After Red Feather nodded his understanding, Jaya spun and left the building. The two swamp dragons hesitated, looking expectantly at Red Feather.

Red Feather turned toward a long wooden table lining one wall. He searched among dozens of clay pots, each painted in bright colors. He withdrew two long yellow fruits from one tall pot and then squatted in front of the swamp dragons. "I know this isn't your favorite, but it's the best I have."

One dragon inched forward and hung its jaw open.

Red Feather placed one fruit inside its mouth.

"By the gods," Frayka whispered. "He's feeding those beasts."

"He's my friend," Greeta whispered back. "He must have good reason." She watched Red Feather, fascinated by his relationship with the animals.

Why wouldn't he be kind to the swamp dragons? Red Feather treated me with the same kindness when I was a dragon.

For a moment, Greeta wondered if he might have bonded with the swamp dragons because he'd been with Greeta when she'd transformed between being mortal and being a dragon. Maybe he thought of the swamp dragons as Greeta's own kind.

The dragon clamped its mouth shut, swishing its tail back and forth.

The other dragon poked its nose at the remaining fruit in Red Feather's hand and knocked it to the floor. It then flicked one paw at the fruit, pushing it away.

The first dragon nudged its way to the second fallen fruit, unable to pick it up from the floor with its teeth. It looked up at Red Feather with hopeful eyes. When it opened its jaw, yellow mush lined its mouth.

Obliging, Red Feather picked up the second fruit from the floor and placed it inside the mushy mouth. Turning to the picky dragon, Red Feather said, "See? Now your friend gets more because you turned your nose up at a perfectly delicious treat."

"Chaca!" Jaya called from outside the stone building. "Zolten!"

The second dragon glared at Red Feather and then skittered away with its companion toward the sound of Jaya's voice.

"Why did you do that, Little Man?" Njall said, standing tall and crossing his arms.

"His name is Red Feather," Greeta said. She bristled at the way Njall mocked Red Feather's diminutive size. "And he doesn't speak Northlander." Turning to Red Feather, she brightened and said, "I'm so happy to see you!" But then she sagged as if carrying a heavy weight. "But my friends are going to die."

Red Feather looked through the pots again. "It looks like Chaca and Zolten took a bite out of your friends. That's why Jaya brought you to me. I can take care of them. Come with me."

Now that her eyes had adjusted to the dim light inside the stone building, Greeta took note of her surroundings. The interior was one room whose ceiling elevated into the building's square cap. Tables crammed with pots lined three sides of the room, and a hearth fire dominated the other side.

Red Feather searched the pots by sniffing at their contents. When he found the right pot, he scooped out a handful of herbs and led Greeta, Frayka, and Njall to the fire. Red Feather poured hot water from a cauldron into two thick wooden bowls, dumped the herbs into each bowl, and then put the steaming bowls aside to steep. Pointing at a bright blue blanket in front of the fire, he said, "Sit."

Greeta obeyed, happy for the chance to rest after a day of walking through the swamp. She gestured for Frayka and Njall to join her. In Northlander, Greeta said, "I think Red Feather can make you feel more comfortable."

Despite the hearth fire, the air felt cooler inside the stone building and no insects bothered her.

While Red Feather busied himself by looking among the contents of the many pots, Greeta couldn't help but notice how different he seemed since the last time she'd seen him, not quite a year ago. His chest and arms appeared more muscular. At the same time, his hands danced among the pots with precision and grace. Red Feather acted like a man with new skills and purpose.

Remembering the way Red Feather had embraced and comforted her when she'd been in her dragon body, Greeta wondered briefly what it would feel like for his hands to dance across her mortal skin. But she shook off that thought.

When she saw Frayka and Njall still standing, Greeta said, "You heard him. Sit!"

Weary from the walk and the wounds, Frayka eased to the ground with Njall's help.

He sat next to her. "We don't understand the little man," Njall said. "And we have no reason to trust him."

"I've known him all my life," Greeta said. "And he saved my life. You have every reason to trust him."

Njall's face scrunched up in disgust. "But why is he so *small*? He stands below our shoulders. Is he still growing?"

"All Shining Star people are small. Red Feather is a normal height for his people." Greeta hesitated. What she had just said wasn't entirely true. "*Almost* normal. His brothers are taller but not by much."

Am I bothered by Red Feather's height?

While growing up in their Shining Star village, Greeta and Wapiti kept pace with each other. Neither ever stood much taller than the other. Once fully grown, Wapiti had the greatest height of any man in the village. He'd felt like an equal.

He'd made Greeta feel normal.

Now, she shifted uneasily and wondered if Wapiti's betrayal had changed her so much that she could never love another man who reminded her of him.

Does Red Feather's size make it impossible for me to love him? Would it make me feel like an outcast because I'm so much taller? Does his resemblance to Wapiti make me think I can't love Red Feather? If I risked giving my heart to him, would he betray me, too? Could Red Feather become as callous as his brother if he had the chance?

After rustling through the supplies in the pots, Red Feather sat next to them with large supple leaves and a handful of gnarled twigs bearing tiny green berries and small leaves with prickly fur on the underside. Placing them aside, Red Feather unwrapped Frayka's bandage and examined her still-bleeding wound.

"That's Chaca's bite." Red Feather pointed at a neat line of bite marks. "She got a solid grip on your friend here."

"Frayka," Greeta said, mustering everything she could to act like her normal self instead of someone debating about her feelings for Red Feather. "Her name is Frayka."

"What?" Frayka said. She stiffened as if bracing herself for terrible news.

Greeta glanced up at Frayka. "I told him your name, that's all."

Turning back to Red Feather, Greeta returned her focus to the important matter at hand: to keep Frayka and Njall from suffering before they died. "Is there anything you can do to help them?"

"Of course!" Red Feather said with a good-natured laugh. "First, the tea should be ready by now. Give that to them to drink and that will alleviate the pain."

Greeta followed his direction. She retrieved the bowls of tea and told her companions to drink. Settling back down on the blanket, she watched Red Feather.

He picked off the green berries, put them into a bowl, and then mashed them into a paste with his fingers. "The fastest way to close up a swamp dragon bite is with needle-nose berries and leaves. Unfortunately, it does hurt."

"Hurt?" His words startled Greeta. "How much?"

Red Feather hesitated, his eyebrows wrinkled in confusion. "They will feel a sharp sting at first, which will get worse throughout the day." He stripped the small leaves with the prickly fur undersides from the twigs and mixed them into the berry paste.

Greeta wrapped her hand around Red Feather's wrist, making him stop. Touching his skin sent a shiver through hers, but Greeta ignored it and kept her focus on the task at hand. "I'm not going to let you hurt these people. It's bad enough that they're going to die. They don't need to suffer any more than they already have."

"Die?" Red Feather's jaw slackened in astonishment. "Who said anything about dying?"

Greeta lowered her voice to a whisper even though she knew Frayka and Njall couldn't understand the Shining Star language she spoke with Red Feather. "Dragons bit them. Everyone knows that once you've been bitten by a dragon your life is over. Everyone knows you have anywhere from hours to a few days to live."

When Red Feather spoke, he matched Greeta's whisper with a gleam in his eye. "Maybe that's true about the dragons in the place where your friends come from." He glanced at Frayka and Njall. "But we're in the Land of Swamp Dragons. If we treat the wounds from a swamp dragon bite within a day after they happen, they heal." He grinned. "Nobody dies under my care."

Astonished, Greeta repressed a sudden urge to take him in her arms and kiss him. Instead, she composed herself, let go of his wrist, and sat back. "How can that be? Are you sure?"

Wearing a buckskin shirt, Red Feather raised it to expose a scar on his chest. Pointing at a huge scar near his waist, Red Feather said, "This happened months ago."

"Look at that!" Njall said.

Sitting next to him, Frayka leaned forward to get a better look. "That looks like a dragon bite." Exchanging a hopeful look with Njall, she said, "If he lives, does he know how we can live, too?"

Staring at the scar, Greeta saw the same outline of teeth that Red Feather had just pointed out on Frayka's wound. She looked at Red Feather in horror. "That dragon you fed. It's the same one that tried to kill you!"

"When Chaca bit me, its intent was to protect Jaya," Red Feather said. "But I knew a few words of Swamp Lander. Enough to tell Jaya I'm from the Shining Star nation and came in peace. When I first met these dragons, they assumed I must be an enemy. But then we got to know each other."

Red Feather cocked his head to one side when he looked at Greeta. "All animals are our brothers and sisters. You know that." Raising an eyebrow, he said, "And you more than anyone else should understand that in a deep way."

Greeta held his gaze, knowing he referred to having witnessed her turn into a dragon. And while his brothers had also seen Greeta shapeshift into a beast, only Red Feather had been by her side when she regained mortal form. Looking at his exposed chest, Greeta remembered how he'd found her naked and the sweetness in the way he'd averted his gaze and ordered his brothers to give her their clothing to wear. Although mortified at the time, Greeta now remembered that day fondly and wished she could go back in time to re-live it.

"Answer me!" Frayka said. "What does this little man know?"

Greeta glanced at Frayka and Njall. "He says he can cure you. He says you'll be fine."

"Fine?" Njall sat up tall and his face regained color. His expression shifted with a multitude of thoughts. "We'll be fine. We're going to live." Njall laughed and waved his hand toward Red Feather.

With new confidence Njall stared at Frayka. "We should get to work on having those children who will inherit your knack for reading portents."

Greeta witnessed the first look of longing pass between Frayka and Njall. The twinge of jealousy Greeta felt at their connection surprised her.

Red Feather ignored the Northlanders and continued his conversation with Greeta. Still holding his shirt up, Red Feather took Greeta's hand in his and placed it against his skin.

His sudden action and the warmth of his chest made Greeta light-headed for a moment.

"It's a scar," Red Feather said. "I recovered. I'm fine. Your friends will be, too."

Still looking into his eyes while Red Feather held her hand against his skin, Greeta felt her neck and shoulders flush.

"Oh, I see," Frayka said. "This little man is your sweetheart."

Njall said, "He can't be her sweetheart! He barely comes up to her knees!"

"Red Feather is a lifelong *friend*." Greeta pulled her hand away from Red Feather's chest. She looked away to keep the North-landers from seeing the truth in her eyes. "Red Feather is my good friend."

Obviously relieved at the chance to heal from the dragon bites, Frayka nudged Njall with a grin. "Look how embarrassed she is! That proves they're sweethearts." She nudged Njall again. "Or on the verge of becoming sweethearts!"

Red Feather let his shirt fall back into place. "What are they saying? Why are they smiling?"

"They're happy they're going to live," Greeta said. She looked into the bowl of needle-nose berries and leaves. "You said that's going to hurt when they eat it?"

"They won't eat it. I'll place it directly on the wounds and then wrap those big white moon leaves around the bites." Red Feather looked from Greeta to the Northland-ers and back to Greeta again as if trying to piece together their relationship. "But yes. It will hurt something awful for the first day or so."

Greeta smiled sweetly. "Then give them extra just to make sure they heal well."

After Red Feather bandaged Frayka's and Njall's wounds, he searched a tall standing pot.

Greeta watched him and worried when his face took a serious expression. "Is something wrong?"

Red Feather cast a troubled glance at

Frayka and Njall. "Perhaps I spoke too soon. I might not have everything I need to heal them."

CHAPTER 14

When Red Feather reached into a tall standing pot and felt the cool touch of its empty bottom, a chill ran through his body. It should have contained ghost grass, the ingredient required to keep Frayka and Njall alive.

How could I have run out of ghost grass? Red Feather thought.

"The key to healing dragon bites is ghost grass," Red Feather told Greeta. Willing himself to stay calm, Red Feather felt all around the inside of the pot but found nothing. He searched in other pots, hoping he'd misplaced his most recent batch of ghost grass.

No luck.

I promised Greeta to heal her friends, but they're going to die without ghost grass. It's late in the season for ghost grass to still be growing. What if I can't find any more?

Greeta stared at him in disbelief.

Red Feather spoke in a calm voice. "We might be able to find some. You can help. But if your friends worry, their fretting could speed up their deaths. We can't let them suspect anything is wrong."

Greeta nodded her understanding.

Red Feather clasped his hands together so no one would see them tremble. He turned to Greeta. "Frayka and Njall need to stay here and rest for several days so I can watch how they heal."

Greeta translated his instructions to her companions, who groaned with pain instead of protesting. Frayka and Njall settled to rest on palettes of straw covered by cloth.

Red Feather picked up an empty bowl. "Come with me," he said to Greeta and walked out of the building.

Greeta hurried to catch up.

"I expect those bites to begin to close their gaps tomorrow," Red Feather said. "That's when they'll need ghost grass. So we need to find some today."

Greeta frowned. "What is ghost grass?"

"It looks like spider webbing but grows like grass." Red Feather pointed to the tall stone columns lining the marketplace. "A vendor might have some."

Red Feather wove his way among the hundreds of people crowding the marketplace and led Greeta to a vendor's stall full of herbs and plant fronds.

He spoke to a woman wearing nothing more than bright paint and many necklaces of crimson and white clay beads. The entire left side of her body sported bright yellow paint while the right side was bright blue. She listened intently to the few words he uttered. She answered with slow and precise words.

Red Feather thanked her and gestured for Greeta to walk by his side.

Keeping up with him, Greeta said, "Are you happier here?"

Surprised, Red Feather turned to look at her. "What?"

Her face lacked expression, which made her look sad. "You seem at home here. People like you. It looks like maybe you've found a new home."

Red Feather's heart beat faster.

Has she missed me? Is she sad because she thinks I'll spend my life here instead of back in our home village?

This was no time to think such thoughts. If they couldn't find ghost grass, Greeta's friends would die.

"I came to Xazaa looking for you," Red Feather said. "I stayed because Shadow said you would come here."

Greeta stared in the distance as if she hadn't heard him. "What did the vendor say? Doesn't she have any ghost grass?"

Red Feather's anxiety grew. "No one has collected any ghost grass since the last full moon. But if I understood what that vendor said, we might be able to collect some outside the city gates." He pointed across the plaza. "This way."

Greeta walked alongside him toward the gate that Jaya had led her through earlier today. "You know their language?"

"Not much. But I'm learning enough to get by."

"How long have you been here? Why are you here? How did you get here?"

Red Feather looked up at Greeta. "Do you remember the day you set sail with those Northlanders?"

"Not by choice!" Greeta protested. "They picked me up and hauled me on board without asking."

Red Feather nodded. "I know. Shadow told me. By the time we ran to the beach the ship had sped away."

"The day you and your brothers brought me back to our village, I ran home and expected to see Papa. But I found Shadow bound by ropes. I freed her and then went to the beach because Shadow said the Northlanders took my family there."

Red Feather nodded, remembering that day. "I met Shadow when she found me and my brothers. She took us to the beach with the hope of helping you. Shadow said she could help by sleeping in your home that night. The next day she said she'd met you in the Dreamtime. Shadow said she'd seen a map and that she knew how to find you. She said she would walk to that place."

Greeta frowned. "But the Northlanders took us away on their ship. You knew we left by sea and sailed away from the Great Turtle Lands. Why did she think she could find me by walking?"

"She didn't," Red Feather said. "Shadow knew where we could find you in the future."

When they approached the city gates, Greeta nudged Red Feather and said, "Will that guard let us pass?"

Before Red Feather could answer, the guard grinned and clapped him on the back in greeting. The guard chatted happily and pointed to a scar on his forearm.

Red Feather paused to examine the scar, nodded his approval, and then shared a laugh with the guard. Red Feather glanced at Greeta. "He fell and got scraped up by a broken stone last week, but the arm is healing nicely."

"You're a healer now?" Greeta said.

The guard stood back and let them pass through the gates.

"I suppose so." Red Feather stepped off the path and into the dense forest. "My uncle back home is a healer. Perhaps it's a skill that runs in my family."

They ducked under tree branches and squeezed between knee-high bushes. Red Feather recognized places where he'd found ghost grass in the recent past, but no more grass grew there. But he knew of a few more places that held promise.

Red Feather paused to touch the leaves of a tree. Broad and shaped like an outstretched hand, the leaves lingered against his skin as if in greeting. "It began when I came looking for you. Remember when they threw me off the cliff?"

"Of course, I remember." Greeta shuddered.

Red Feather thought back to last year when Greeta's father asked him to take his brothers and search when she went missing. Red Feather eventually learned Greeta had been kidnapped in her own land by members of the Shining Star nation. He still remembered the look of relief on her face when Red Feather and his brothers confronted the men who captured her. But those men tied up the brothers after hurling Red Feather from a mountainside in a fall that should have spelled certain death.

"You never told me how you survived," Greeta said.

"I landed on very high and dense bushes. They caught me when I fell." Red Feather smiled. "They lowered me onto the ground. And when I thanked them, the way they moved made me think they understood me. I kept talking and they moved their leaves to answer." He gestured to the vegetation surrounding them. "And now I do it every day."

Red Feather worried. They'd been searching for a good while now, and he saw no trace of ghost grass anywhere. If he understood the Swamp Landers correctly, ghost grass grew for brief periods of time throughout the year.

But once it stopped growing, months would pass before it would sprout again.

He stopped at a tree trunk and used his thumb to scrape a dollop of sap oozing from its gaping bark to the bowl he carried. "This black sap helps most plants to work better at healing." He slipped the sap into a small container hanging from his belt. If he couldn't find ghost grass, maybe this sap would help to keep the Northlanders alive long enough for him to go far beyond the city and search remote places for ghost grass.

"But what about when you first came here?" Greeta said. "How did the Swamp Landers find out you can heal?"

"Shadow brought us through the swamps, but Jaya and her dragons surprised us. When Chaca bit me, I yelled. A needle-nose plant turned its leaves and berries toward me, and I took them. I pressed them against the wound and felt better right away. The way I recognized and used the plant surprised Jaya. I think because Xazaa needed more healers and she didn't expect me to be one. She took us to the city. On the way there a patch of ghost grass rustled at me, so I picked some. I used it when I changed the dressing and healed up nicely."

It's no use. All the ghost grass has been gathered or eaten by animals or withered away to nothing.

Red Feather stopped and looked at Greeta. "I must tell you something."

Greeta stood still and gazed into his eyes. "What?"

"The ghost grass is gone. There is no more."

Greeta paled. "How can you give up so easily? There must be more!"

Red Feather's heart sank. He didn't want to hurt Greeta, but he couldn't lie to her either. "Your friends need ghost grass to cure the bite. I thought I had plenty of ghost grass on hand, but it's all gone. I thought we could find it here, but there's none left." He squeezed her hands. "The last thing I wanted was to fail you."

He assumed she would cry, but Greeta returned his strong grasp instead.

Looking up to meet his gaze, Greeta said, "Tell me what it smells like."

Perplexed, Red Feather shook his head. "What do you mean?"

"The ghost grass. What kind of odor does it have?"

Red Feather's heart sank even deeper at Greeta's unwarranted hope.

This is my fault. I gave her that hope before I knew it to be false.

"It has no odor," Red Feather said.

He flinched when Greeta squeezed his hands tight.

"Everything has an odor," Greeta insisted. "Last year when I turned into a dragon, something happened to me. I understood things by smelling them. I would flick out my dragon tongue and all kinds of information would land on it. But it wasn't taste. I used my tongue to gather smells!"

Now Red Feather worried about her. Whoever heard of smelling things with one's tongue? It made no sense.

Greeta is panicking.

"I'm not panicking," Greeta said.

When Red Feather started at her words, she smiled and said, "I could smell what you were feeling." Still squeezing his hands, she added, "And who are you to doubt me when you have such a peculiar relationship with plants? You think you can communicate with them but that I can't detect where they are by the way they smell?"

"It smells light," Red Feather said, giving into her wishes before he realized it.

Gathering his thoughts, he said, "Like the white flowers back home that blossom through the snow at the end of winter."

Greeta let go of his hands. She stood tall, inhaling the jungle air, thick with warm humidity. She then dropped to her hands and knees. She lowered her face to the ground and breathed deeply. After a short while, she looked up at Red Feather. "I've picked up its trail," Greeta said.

She climbed back to her feet and ran through the jungle with Red Feather on her heels. Every so often she stopped to inhale and then head in a new direction.

Finally, Greeta stopped and pointed at the ground.

Red Feather knelt in front of a patch of delicate white grass, so fine that the blades looked almost transparent. "We have wounded people who need you," he said to the grass. "Who is willing to help today?"

The grass closest to his hand leaned into it. The blades nestled against his skin.

"I thank you," Red Feather said. He plucked the grass from the ground.

Relief washed through Red Feather. This bit of ghost grass would be enough to save the lives of the Northlanders and keep Greeta from being disappointed in him.

Even better, her friends wouldn't need the ghost grass until tomorrow. They could take their time returning to Xazaa.

Thunder rumbled overhead.

Red Feather looked skyward and beamed. "Wonderful! We're desperate for rain." Standing, he gestured for Greeta to follow when he ran back toward the path. "Hurry! Let me show you something remarkable!"

CHAPTER 15

Bewildered by Red Feather's excitement, Greeta followed him out of the dense forest and back onto the dirt path outside the city.

"The city of Xazaa is located far away from rivers, and swamp water isn't safe to drink." Red Feather rubbed his shoe against the dirt path, revealing porous white rock beneath. "But the only rock in this region is like this. Watch what happens in the rain."

The skies opened up above them, letting loose a brief but drenching shower. Several minutes later the rain stopped, leaving droplets on the foliage surrounding them. Red Feather pointed at the ground.

The sudden storm left large puddles along the dirt path. But while Greeta watched, the ground seemed to drink the standing water and it disappeared before her eyes.

Greeta knelt and touched the ground where a large puddle had stood moments ago. The dirt felt damp. She pushed it aside to reveal the pocked white rock underneath. She saw no sign of water.

"It runs through the rock," Red Feather said. "That means you can't carve any containers for the rain out of this rock because it can't hold water. How do you think so many people can live in this city without a river or safe water to drink?"

"I don't know."

Red Feather grinned. "Follow me." He raced along the dirt path and through the city gates with a wave to the guard.

The expansive white plazas stood deserted. Greeta assumed the throngs of people sought shelter from the rain, now coming down lightly in the city.

The thick gray clouds and the darkened sky made the city's large crimson flat-top pyramid and the buildings surrounding it look ominous.

"Look at the channels," Red Feather said. He pointed at the white stone plazas covering the entire city grounds.

For the first time Greeta saw the narrow channels carved in the stone. Those channels ran in different lines and directions throughout the city. Just a few steps away, one channel ran toward the setting sun. Narrower than Greeta's forearm, the channel guided the rushing water away. All the water on the plazas appeared to fall into channels and run away like tiny rivers throughout the city.

Red Feather gestured for Greeta to follow. He walked alongside the nearby channel running west.

"I don't understand," Greeta said, filled with hope at this new and unexpected opportunity to know more about Red Feather. "You said all the rock is like the one you showed me. The water ran straight through it. What kind of magic keeps that from happening here?"

"It's not magic. It's cleverness." He swept his hands across the plazas surrounding them. "They make a paste with powdered stone and minerals. They spread the paste on top of the stone and let it dry. Once dry, it repels water. There is enough rain for the crops, but they had to find a way to store water to drink."

Within minutes they reached the end of the channel. It led to a small lake on the outskirts of town.

"They're adding water to a lake?" Greeta said.

"No." Red Feather grinned in delight. "First, they carved out a deep basin in the stone. Then they covered it with plaster so it could collect water. This wasn't a lake that they found. It's a lake they created.

They built lakes all around the city."

Greeta marveled at the sight before her. It looked like a real lake. But even in the dim twilight, the water looked pale instead of dark. Squinting, she thought she could detect the bright white stone beneath the lake.

Red Feather's enthusiasm for the people of Xazaa and their creations surprised Greeta.

What do I really know about Red Feather?

Although she'd known Red Feather all her life, Greeta always thought of him simply as one of many brothers to her former sweetheart, Wapiti. She'd considered Red Feather as a future brother-in-law but rarely saw him outside of his large family. For the first time, Greeta realized she didn't know much about what made Red Feather happy or content or excited.

How could I have spent so much of my life being around Red Feather and understanding so little about him? Was I so blinded by my love for Wapiti that I noticed so little about others?

She looked up at Red Feather, fascinated by his open enthusiasm for the people who had captured him. "You like the Swamp Landers."

"Of course," Red Feather said. "They built a city far greater than anything the legends about them ever mentioned. The way they store water is just one of their many wonders. And if it hadn't been for Shadow asking for my help in finding you, I never would have known such wonders exist."

A new thought made Greeta uneasy. "Where is Shadow?"

Red Feather's face became still and solemn. "Working with their shamans."

"Why is she working with them?" Greeta's unease began to feel like panic. "I thought you and Shadow came here because she said you would find me here in the future. And you have. So why isn't she here?"

Red Feather glanced at the darkening sky. "We should go back while we can see our way." He walked back toward his healing building.

"Wait!" Greeta hurried to catch up with him. "We came here looking for Finehurst. He's a threat to us all. Does Shadow know that? Do the Swamp Dragon shamans know about Finehurst?"

"I don't know." Red Feather gave the sky another worried look. "You'll have to find Shadow and ask her yourself."

They hurried through the dark city. When they passed between the pyramid and an opposing column on the border of the marketplace, Greeta thought she saw something move in the shadows.

No, not the shadows. It's something on

the column that's moving.

Greeta paused to stare at the column. The image carved into it seemed to crawl across the stone.

It can't be the image moving. It must be a lizard or a snake.

Frightened, Greeta sprinted to catch up with Red Feather and ran into the safety of the building as the last hint of light disappeared.

CHAPTER 16

The next morning Greeta woke up feeling stiff after sleeping on a stone floor.

Rays of early morning sunlight streamed through openings and gave the interior of the stone building a pale yellow glow. The air smelled clean and damp. Sitting up, Greeta looked around to see Njall snoring and Frayka sleeping by his side on Red Feather's bed of straw and blankets in a nearby corner.

At the far end of the building, Red Feather busied himself over a crackling fire. Within minutes, he brought three plain clay cups of steaming tea with him. After handing one to Greeta, he placed the other cups on a ledge. "Wake up," he said to Njall and Frayka. "It's time to check your wounds."

Frayka spoke with her face still buried

against the blanket. "Why does Little Man talk at us? Can't he see we're sleeping?"

Remembering the way Frayka and Njall had teased her without mercy, Greeta decided to have some fun with them. Speaking in Northlander, Greeta said, "Whenever Red Feather speaks, you should assume he wants to look at your wounds to make sure you're healing properly. And if you don't do as he says, he'll bring back his friends to make sure you obey."

"Friends?" Njall said. Squinting and groggy-eyed, he sat up and rubbed his face. "What friends?"

"The swamp dragons." Greeta sipped her tea.

Frayka bolted upright, her hair resembling a rat's nest. She pushed it away from her eyes. "He wouldn't dare."

"We're in the Land of Swamp Dragons." Greeta kept her voice calm and matter-of-fact. "We're in their land, not yours. Red Feather has made friends with the people here, and he speaks their language. So do what he says unless you want to become supper for dragons."

Red Feather stepped between them, handing tea to Frayka and Njall, who accepted with glares of indignation. "What did you tell them?" Red Feather said.

"Something to keep them in line," Greeta said. "I expect them to be more cooperative now."

Red Feather retrieved several large leaves and a bowl of mashed herbs and berries from the nearest table. "Let's find out." He pointed at Frayka. "What is this one's name again?"

"Frayka."

Red Feather knelt and looked at the Northlander. "Frayka," he said to her. He gestured at her injured foot.

Frayka responded with an annoyed snort, but she placed her foot in his hands.

After un-wrapping the bandage Red Feather had placed around her foot the previous day, he beamed. Pointing at her much improved wound, Red Feather said, "This is healing very well."

Daring to look at her foot, its improvement surprised Frayka so much that she forgot to be angry. Smiling at Red Feather, she said, "Look! It's better!"

Greeta struggled to keep from laughing at Frayka's sudden change of heart.

Excited, Frayka turned to look at Greeta. "Do you see this? Your little man made my foot heal so fast!"

"You're not healed yet," Greeta said. "And his name is Red Feather."

Red Feather looked up at the mention of his name.

"Red Feather," Frayka repeated.

Red Feather smiled at her. "Frayka," he said.

"This is good," Frayka said to Greeta. "Now we speak each other's language."

This time Greeta couldn't help but laugh.

Red Feather gestured for Frayka to drink her tea, and she obeyed.

"Good," she said in a loud voice, as if to help Red Feather understand her better. "Red Feather, this tastes good."

Red Feather gave a quizzical glance to Greeta.

"She likes your tea," Greeta translated.

Red Feather looked back at Frayka with a smile and a nod.

A pang of jealousy surprised Greeta. She didn't like the way Red Feather and Frayka looked at each other. She'd been happier when Frayka had been angry at him.

Nonsense. Frayka's just warming up to him. There's nothing to worry about.

Njall scrambled to sit close to Frayka and then draped his arm around her shoulder. "Tell Little Man to stay away from my Frayka."

I'm not the only one who noticed Frayka's change of heart.

Greeta cleared her throat. "Njall says..."

"No need," Red Feather said.

Following Red Feather's gaze at Njall, Greeta recognized the irritation in Red Feather's eyes and Njall's protective glare.

Red Feather focused on applying more

of his healing paste to Frayka's wound. He covered it with ghost grass and wrapped fresh leaves around the wound. "I know exactly what he means."

Greeta caught Njall's glance and gave him a smile and nod. For the first time she forgave his past cruelties toward Frayka and wanted his new affection for her to grow.

Njall nodded his thanks but kept a close watch on every move Red Feather made.

Once finished attending to Frayka, Red Feather spent extra time and care tending Njall's wound. To Greeta he said, "Tell them they need to spend today resting here."

Greeta translated. Once more, she added her own advice that if Frayka and Njall didn't obey they'd have to answer to the swamp dragons.

"Fine," Frayka said. Handing her clay cup to Red Feather, she said very loudly, "More tea. And food. I'm starving."

After leaving the Northlanders well supplied with food and drink, Greeta and Red Feather walked out of the healing building and into the day.

"I need to find Shadow," Greeta said. "I need to know why she knew I'd come to this city and what it means."

Red Feather said, "When Shadow left, she told me to have patience and to fit in with the people here. I've done as she asked, but I've also tried to find out what happened to her. No one can tell me where she is. We arrived last fall." Red Feather glanced back at his building. "When winter began, the Swamp Landers put me there and let me gather healing supplies."

"What does Jaya know?"

Red Feather gave Greeta a pointed look. "Have you not noticed that Jaya doesn't say much? I have already tried asking her."

"Maybe now that I'm here things will be different. Maybe Shadow has been waiting for me to come."

Red Feather mulled over her words. "All right. We should talk to the vendors in the marketplace. They seem to know everything that happens here."

Walking through the bustling city, Greeta remembered the strange sight she witnessed in the dark last night: the movement of a carved image crawling across its stone. Now she craned her neck and looked up at the buildings and columns surrounding her, all covered in carvings of shapes, mortal faces, and animals. A square border contained each carving as if it were caged.

Noticing her interest, Red Feather explained the images to her. "You can tell the purpose of each structure by the illustrations that decorate it. My building is covered with carvings of herbs and plants and berries along with the faces of men and women. That tells you it's a place of healing."

He then pointed at a squat and round building perched on a high stone platform to their right. "See the stars and the moon carved into the base of that building? It's where the Swamp Lander Sky Watchers study the movement of the stars. And they use those lines and dots carved next to the stars and moon to figure out the best times to plant each year."

Greeta squinted at him. "How can such lines and dots tell you that?"

Red Feather grinned. "The Sky Watchers say when the rays of the rising sun illuminate all of those carvings, it's time to plant. This is a time determined by the Swamp Landers' ancestors many generations ago."

Making progress toward the market, Greeta shivered when she saw the columns flanking its entrance.

"What troubles you?" Red Feather said, his brow creasing with worry.

"I saw something strange last night." Greeta shrugged. "Maybe it was only my imagination."

"Tell me what you saw." When Greeta hesitated, Red Feather said, "Please."

If anyone else from her village had asked, Greeta would have laughed it off and claimed she'd seen nothing more than an animal crawling on the column. Because Red Feather had been a loyal and unquestioning friend when she'd transformed into a dragon and then back into mortal form again, she trusted him. "I saw something on one of those columns. I thought I saw the carving come out of the stone and crawl across it."

Red Feather responded with a solemn nod. "I've never seen anything out of place, but I've heard people talk about strange things happening in the city at night. They talk of ghosts. It's why no one walks the streets after the sun sets." He stared at each column. "Each column looks as it should. Nothing seems out of place."

Greeta followed his gaze. Sure enough, all of the images looked intact. She saw no missing images or anything that looked out of place. "Maybe I imagined it."

"Perhaps not." Red Feather rested his hand on her back. "I can talk to people who have mentioned ghosts. Maybe they've seen the carvings move. But until then I think we should keep what you saw to ourselves."

When they entered the marketplace, Greeta cast one last glance at the columns. Although none of the carvings moved, she felt no satisfaction.

Instead, she felt a chilling dread.

CHAPTER 17

Greeta followed Red Feather all day. They agreed on a two-fold mission. Working their way from vendor to vendor through the marketplace, Red Feather asked if anyone knew where to find Jaya with the intent of asking her if she knew what had happened to Shadow. His second task involved quizzing vendors about ghosts or any other peculiar things they might know about what could happen in the city after dark.

By mid-day they completed their way through the marketplace with disappointing information to show for their efforts.

"They all say the same thing about Jaya," Red Feather said. "An important ceremony will happen later today. They say Jaya's place is by the king's side."

"King?" Greeta said. She knew of no

such word in either the Shining Star language or the Northlander language. "What is a king?"

"Their ruler." Red Feather gestured toward the flat-top pyramid rising high at the city's center. From where they stood among other buildings and towering trees dotting the avenues, they could see only the uppermost platform of the pyramid. "He lives there with his family. He shows himself only when he has something important to say."

"He rules the Swamp Landers?"

Red Feather shook his head. "Only this city. Only Xazaa. They tell me there are many cities, which make up the swamp lands. No one rules the Land of Swamp Dragons. Instead, each city has its own king. But this is the grandest city."

Greeta considered the situation. Her first concern was to find Shadow. "Did you ask them about Shadow? Did anyone know where to find her?"

Red Feather shook his head once more. "Shadow didn't stay here for long. Few people saw her. Most don't know she exists. No one I asked knew who I was talking about. I only know the merchants. In a city of this size, I'm lucky to know anyone."

"But talking to Jaya is the best way to find out where we can find Shadow."

"I believe so."

Greeta cleared her throat, suddenly aware of how nervous she felt to ask the next question. "Did you also ask the merchants about ghosts?"

"Of course!" Red Feather laughed. "Didn't you notice how long most of those conversations lasted? My question about Shadow took only a moment for them to answer. The rest of the time they were telling me their ghost stories!"

The amusement faded from his eyes, making him look more somber. "But none of their stories sounded anything like what you saw. Most are about how they see the ghost of a dead relative wandering through the crops or at the edge of the city at night. I am not convinced you saw a ghost."

Assuming he doubted her, Greeta felt herself become prickly. "I know what I saw!"

"I understand." Red Feather reached up to place a gentle hand on her shoulder. "But perhaps a carving that comes to life is not the same as a ghost. Perhaps it is caused by something else."

Red Feather's touch made Greeta feel relaxed and nervous at the same time. His friendship calmed her, but the thought of being held in his arms flashed through Greeta's thoughts like a welcome summer day. She shook that thought away. They had critical tasks at hand, and such flights of fantasy would have to wait for another time. "If it's not a ghost," Greeta said, "what can it be?"

"I don't know." Red Feather let his hand drift away from Greeta's shoulder. "But I think we should be here when the king appears. All the merchants say it is something we should not miss."

"And what do we do until then?" For a moment, Greeta imagined spending the rest of the day strolling through the city, hand in hand with Red Feather.

He glanced up at the sun, squinting in its bright light dominating a clear sky. "Looks like we have enough time to check on your friends. They're healing, but they looked too pale this morning." He looked back at Greeta. "Frayka and ..."

"Njall," Greeta said.

Red Feather gave her a blank look. "Nal?" he said, trying to sound out the name by himself.

"Knee-yawl," Greeta said, placing the emphasis on "knee." She understood how strange some of the Northlander names must sound to him. She'd heard them all her life from Papa and Auntie Peppa, but most Shining Star people had never heard such names before. Except for those belonging to Greeta and her family.

"Knee-yawl," Red Feather repeated. Then he said it faster: "Njall."

Greeta smiled and nodded her approval.

"So we go back to check on the wounded."

They made their way through the city streets until they reached the healing building. Once inside, Red Feather made preparations to change the dressings for each dragon bite, while Frayka and Njall peppered him with questions that he couldn't understand.

Greeta opted to answer instead of translating the questions for Red Feather. "We spent the morning trying to find Shadow."

"Shadow?" Frayka said, frowning in disapproval. "Who is Shadow?"

"A Shining Star woman," Greeta said. "She acted as my guide before your father took my family to the Land of Ice. She told Red Feather they would find me in the Land of Swamp Dragons, so they traveled here together. If anyone can help us get out of here, it's Shadow."

"But we're here to find Finehurst and kill him so he hurts no one else," Njall said.

"No!" Greeta protested. "We're here to get the rest of the tapestry from him so he won't be able to use it to hurt anyone again. We never said anything about killing him!"

Njall nudged Frayka, who sat next to him on the floor. "We never said we *wouldn't* kill him."

Frayka smirked while Njall laughed out loud.

"Why do they laugh?" Red Feather said, casting a curious glance from one Northlander to the other.

Greeta heaved an exasperated sigh. "They're talking about killing Finehurst. Assuming we can find him, that is."

Red Feather returned his attention to wrapping fresh leaves around Frayka's wound. "That might not be such a bad idea."

"Red Feather!" Greeta cried, astonished that any member of the Shining Star nation would consider such a violent act.

"Finehurst acts like a rogue bear," Red Feather said. "If he endangers the lives of others, we must consider all solutions for keeping him from harming the next seven generations." Looking at Greeta, he added, "Not to mention our own."

Still troubled, Greeta said, "But you talk about taking a life."

"As a last course of action," Red Feather said.

Greeta thought about the dragon and dragon eggs she'd discovered in the cavern beneath Finehurst's home in the Great Turtle Lands. She still worried Finehurst would use them in some horrible way. She'd failed to thwart Finehurst when she first met him, but Greeta believed the only thing that would have worked would have been to kill him.

Her thoughts shifted to the people of the

Shining Star nation and everything she'd learned from them. "But we don't kill people."

Red Feather finished tending to Frayka and shifted his attention to re-dressing Njall's wound. "Are you so quick to forget that Finehurst tried to kill me?"

Greeta's body tightened at the memory of Red Feather being thrown off a cliff by one of Finehurst's men. Red Feather's life had been saved only by the grace of vegetation that caught his fall. Disturbed by the memory of his brush with death, her voice softened to a whisper. "I didn't forget."

"And you feel no need to avenge what they did to me?"

"Revenge is pointless," Greeta said. She focused on everything she'd learned from the Shining Star people, because it contradicted the feelings she remembered having when she'd been a dragon. "It solves nothing except to fan a fire that should be put out."

Red Feather paused to glance at her with a smile. "And Finehurst is that fire. I suggest you think now about what you're willing and not willing to do to Finehurst in order to protect yourself and the rest of us."

Frayka interrupted. "What are you saying about Finehurst? Don't leave us out!"

Switching to speak Northlander, Greeta

said, "We're talking about whether or not to kill Finehurst."

Frayka gave Greeta a blank stare. "Of course we're going to kill him. Why else would we leave the Land of Ice and suffer dragon bites?"

Red Feather grinned. "Greeta, I believe we all agree that you are too soft-hearted."

Astonished, Greeta gazed at all of them. To Red Feather, she said, "When did you learn how to speak Northlander?"

"I don't." Red Feather returned his attention to Njall. "But Frayka's face says it all."

"He's talking about me now," Frayka said. "What did he say?"

"He agrees with you." Greeta concentrated on switching back and forth between the two languages. To Red Feather she said, "Why do you think I'm too soft-hearted?"

Nodding his approval at the progress of Njall's healing, Red Feather changed the dressing. "Because like every other living thing in this world, you have a right to be here," Red Feather said to Greeta. "But unlike every other living thing in this world, you don't seem to understand that you also have the right to fight for yourself. To protect yourself. And sometimes when you protect yourself, you kill another living thing. You aren't willing to do that."

"But they talk about killing Finehurst," Greeta said. "Northlanders like these don't hesitate to slaughter people. We don't murder people."

"But we kill animals."

Greeta shrugged off his argument. "We kill animals for food. And we always give thanks to the animal for giving its life to feed us and allow us to stay alive."

Red Feather stared at her. "But isn't every animal our brother or sister? Don't animals have just as much right to live as we do?"

Greeta kept silent, considering Red Feather's words.

All her life, Greeta thought she understood Red Feather. But now his words gave her pause.

Have I failed to understand what I learned by growing up in a Shining Star village? Our people do everything possible to avoid killing people, and we always succeed.

Is Red Feather saying there might be a time and a reason to commit murder?

Am I the only mortal in this world who doesn't believe in killing? If I don't change what I believe, could it cost me my life?

And if I do change what I believe, how can I live with myself?

When finished tending to Njall, Red Feather stood and faced Greeta. "I suggest you think now about what you're willing and not willing to do to Finehurst for the sake of protecting yourself and the rest of us. Otherwise, it might be too easy for him to kill you."

Startled, Greeta nodded her understanding. The depth of concern in Red Feather's eyes scared her. "I will think about it," she promised.

CHAPTER 18

By the time Red Feather finished re-dressing the Northlanders' dragon bites, the sunlight streaming through the window openings formed long and angular shapes on the floor.

Red Feather pointed at them. "The day grows late." Rushing to an opening, he placed his hands on the stone sill and leaned out. "Everyone has come in from the fields. They're walking toward the pyramid. We should go."

Greeta pointed at Frayka and Njall. "What about them? Should they stay here? Or can they come with us?"

"Whatever they like." Red Feather turned to face Greeta. "But I believe we should leave now."

Like children anxious to play outside after a long winter, Frayka and Njall quickly decided to join the trek from the healing building to the pyramid in the city center and arrived in time to claim seats on a low stone wall running alongside an avenue.

On each side of the pyramid, a row of people wearing bright yellow, blue, white, and green paint on their bodies sat with their backs to its base. Each man and woman wore a different design made up of straight lines, jagged lines, dots, or images similar to the carvings on buildings and other structures throughout the city. Some people held a drum, whistle, or bone flute, while others sat empty-handed.

"Who are they?" Greeta whispered to Red Feather.

"Musicians and dancers," he said. "I've seen them at other gatherings."

Thousands of people jammed the avenues surrounding the pyramid. Most smelled like stale sweat after having spent the day working in the fields surrounding the city.

The edge of the jungle stood behind the fields. Although the sun still hung slightly above the tree line, thin clouds took on the tinge of pink and accepted the inevitability of sunset.

The sun's low rays struck the city buildings and cast long and deep shadows among the throngs of people gathering around the base of the pyramid. Noticing how some standing in the shadows shivered, Greeta felt grateful to be sitting in the warmth of the sun.

A man shouted and pointed at the top platform of the pyramid.

The crowd cheered when Jaya emerged from the house on the highest platform, flanked by her two dragons. She wore a fresh headdress of green vines and purple flowers. White paint covered her face, but instead of brown dots she now wore vertical streaks of red across her cheeks.

The musicians and dancers on the street level stood and performed. They sang while marching and dancing around the base of the pyramid.

A staircase bisected each of the pyramid's four sides. Jaya and her dragons descended the staircase facing Greeta. The dragons took care with the steepness of the steps coming down from the top platform. But soon they delighted at the shallower steps they encountered and scampered down the rest of the stairway. Jaya took more time by keeping an even gait.

When Jaya neared the bottom of the pyramid, Red Feather nudged Greeta and pointed at Jaya.

A few hummingbirds darted around the purple flowers covering Jaya's head.

Still singing, the musicians and dancers returned to stand with their backs against the pyramid, making room for Jaya and the swamp dragons.

A sudden movement caught the corner of Greeta's eye. She looked to her left but saw nothing out of place. The city's residents packed every avenue. People sat on every available space. A young man climbed one of the carved columns by the entrance to the marketplace and sat on top of it. The columns stood in the sun, and the young man shaded his eyes with his hands to watch the pyramid.

Jaya glided down from the last step of the pyramid and turned to look up at its top platform. The two swamp dragons circled her feet.

The musicians and dancers fell silent.

The king emerged from his home on the top platform of the pyramid. He wore only a white linen loincloth. Gold jewelry sparkled across his body. Chains of gold wrapped below each knee. Bands of gold encircled his arms. Large gold hoops adorned his ears. A massive necklace made of gold hammered into the shape of a pyramid covered his chest. A sun-bleached animal skull rested on top of the king's head, and a spray of large and colorful feathers surrounded his neck and head. He held a long staff topped by a stone ax blade.

The king spoke, pointing at the sky.

"What is he saying?" Greeta whispered to Red Feather.

Red Feather strained to listen to the

king. "I can't understand much. I think he said something about rain."

Greeta sat back to let Red Feather listen. She scanned the crowd around the pyramid. Everyone appeared spellbound by the king's words.

Once more, something at the edge of her vision moved. When Greeta turned to look for it, she ended up looking at the young man sitting on top of the column.

Could that be the column where I saw something strange last night? Something that might or might not be a ghost?

The king spoke again, and the crowd buzzed in response.

Greeta looked back at the pyramid. She said to Red Feather, "I don't understand. What is everyone so excited about?"

He pointed at the steps in front of them. "You see how the pyramid is painted red but its steps are white?"

Greeta nodded.

"Look at the edge of the stairway closest to us. Look at the edge that runs from the ground to the top."

An undulating darkness ran alongside the stairs. It reminded her of the dark shadow she'd seen in the city last night.

"Don't worry," Red Feather said. "It's a shadow. If I understood the king correctly, it happens on this same day each year. I think he said it's thc serpent god telling them the best time to plant the new crops."

The undulation was indeed a shadow. Several sunbeams pierced through tall trees. When the tree branches moved in the wind, they crossed the rays of the sun, which made the shadow appear to move. Turning to Frayka and Njall, Greeta explained the phenomenon to them.

Njall grinned with appreciation. "It looks like a giant black serpent is crawling down the stairway!"

Another movement caught Greeta's attention. Once more, she looked at the column near the marketplace entrance.

This time the young man sitting on top jerked away from the edge as if something had just scared him.

The carving that covered the column shivered. Black lines crawled across the surface until they formed the life-size image of a man.

Greeta recognized him immediately.

"Finehurst!" Greeta shouted. She stood on top of the wall where she'd been sitting and pointed at the column. "Finehurst!"

She reached for her sword only to remember that since arriving in the city she'd left it at Red Feather's healing building. Looking at Frayka, she cried, "Dagger!"

But Frayka had already seen and recognized Finehurst's image. With dagger in hand, she launched off the wall and into the crowd, shoving people aside in an attempt to get to the column.

"Give me your dagger!" Greeta said to Njall.

Njall held up a hand in protest. "What's happening? Where is Frayka going?"

Desperate, Greeta took hold of the grip of the dagger tucked under Njall's belt and pulled it out herself. Jumping into the crowd, she shouted, "Out of my way!"

Frayka thrust her dagger at the black lines on its surface. Unlike the undulating shadow serpent on the pyramid, Finehurst's image darted inside the frame of the column's edges. But it also appeared to laugh at Frayka's efforts.

"You kidnapped the man who must father my children!" Frayka shouted at the ethereal image floating against the face of the column. She stabbed at the darting image as if trying to pin down a fly. "You try to ruin everything! I will not let you!"

The throng of people surrounding the column stared in wide-eyed fear at Frayka and edged away from her. Because all avenues and streets were still crowded with the city's entire population, they could only take a step or two away. The rest of the crowd still buzzed at the sight of the shadow of the serpent on the pyramid, unaware of Frayka, Greeta, and the moving image on the column.

Greeta shoved her way through the

crowd. Like the ocean, it had its own motion, powerful and strong. So many people packed tightly together meant that any sudden move made by one person would ripple like a wave. She kept a tight grip on Njall's dagger and held it with the point down to make sure no one would get hurt, especially if a sudden ripple hit Greeta from behind.

Steps behind Frayka, Greeta paused to look at Finehurst's image. The black lines now looked like smoke rising from the stone surface instead of skimming across it.

"No!" Frayka cried out, jabbing at the air above her head.

The people watching her shouted and pointed at the black cloud of smoke forming above the column. Within minutes a hush fell over the hundreds of people standing closest to the pyramid. The thousands on the outskirts still hummed with excitement.

The smoke transformed into the shape of a long ribbon, struck at Greeta, and wrapped around her like a shroud.

Enveloped inside the black smoke, Greeta tried to raise Njall's dagger, but her arm wouldn't move. Confused, she tried again, but her arm still refused to budge.

This makes no sense.

Greeta took a different tack. She tried to step through the black fog surrounding her, but it wouldn't let her. No matter how hard she tried to shift her position, her body remained still.

Panic made Greeta's heart pound, and she panted for breath. The acrid scent of smoke burned her nose, and she coughed.

I'm going to die! Finehurst is killing me!

Terrified, Greeta tried to scream, but she couldn't open her mouth or make a sound.

Then a new thought struck her.

I'm a dragon girl.

Greeta remembered the power she'd felt when in the shape of a dragon. She remembered the ease with which she'd moved through the land, knowing everything could be hers for the taking. She remembered her disinterest in mortals and how insignificant they seemed to her.

Why should her feelings about mortals be any different than her feelings about this black smoke?

Confidence and determination crept like a fever throughout her body. Greeta relished the touch of the black smoke against her skin because it would be so easy to devour.

I can destroy you, Finehurst. Right now.

As if reading her mind, the force that locked Greeta's body in place vanished in an instant.

Although still in mortal form, an animalistic fury rushed through Greeta's veins. She opened her mouth wide and snapped at the black smoke still wrapped around her. But before she could bite, the smoke blasted high above her reach and zipped toward Jaya, who stood at the bottom of the pyramid stairs.

"Jaya!" Greeta shouted in a warning voice.

Jaya looked up and the expression drained from her face when she saw the smoke. It wrapped around her head. Jaya flailed her arms and tried to push the smoke away from her face. Instead, her hands simply pushed through it.

"It's smothering her!" Greeta shouted. She shouldered her way through the crowd, but every step felt like pushing a boulder uphill. The onlookers surrounding the pyramid screamed and tried to run away, but too many people jammed the avenues.

The two dragons drew themselves upright and steadied their front paws on Jaya's shoulders and back. The animals snapped at the smoke that encircled her head.

When Greeta pushed through the edge of the crowd surrounding Jaya, the smoke broke free. Taking the shape of a dragon, it attacked the shadow of the serpent descending the pyramid. The smoke dragon clamped its jaws around the neck of the serpent shadow and wrenched it free from the stone stairway.

Greeta stared at the sight, not understanding what she saw. "That's impossible," she said. "You can't do that to a shadow."

The smoke dragon sped halfway up the long stone stairway, taking the serpent shadow with it. The smoke dragon jerked its head until the neck of the serpent shadow snapped. The smoke dragon flung the serpent shadow down the steps of the pyramid.

When the serpent shadow struck the last few steps, it fell into another shadow now cast by the sun at the base of the pyramid and vanished.

Jaya screamed. Her dragons pushed away from her and fell back to all fours. They nosed the shadow where the serpent had disappeared.

The smoke dragon climbed the stairway toward the king, still standing tall at the entrance to his home at the top of the pyramid.

The king shouted and held his ax-blade staff with both hands, ready to fight the attacker.

Still screaming, Jaya raced up the stairs on the heels of the smoke dragon. Her own dragons hurried to tackle the steep incline but couldn't keep up.

The king yelled and delivered cutting blows through the air between him and the ethereal creature that threatened him.

The smoke dragon came to a halt before the king. It wound its head from side to side, seeming to size up the man standing before it.

Greeta became aware of her tight grip on Njall's dagger, not knowing what to do.

Running at a slower pace, Jaya was now only several steps behind the tip of the smoke dragon's whipping tail.

She's struggling. Jaya is running out of breath.

Just as it had done with the serpent shadow, the smoke dragon lunged at the king and clamped its jaws around his neck.

Shrieking in pain, the king managed to wave his staff through the smoke dragon's body although the blows had no effect.

Jaya launched herself up the final steps and threw herself at the smoke dragon. She reached out to tackle its lower legs, but she passed through its body and landed on the platform near the king.

The smoke dragon jumped up to the top of the king's house, taking the king with him. Once more, the smoke dragon wrenched its head from side to side until the king's neck snapped. The smoke dragon let the king's body fall from its jaws onto the roof.

With a scream, Jaya fell to her knees. Hauling themselves up to the top platform, the two dragons circled close around her.

The smoke dragon flew over the city and its fields to disappear in the surrounding jungle.

Someone near Greeta shouted and pointed at her. Within moments, a throng of enraged Swamp Landers cornered Greeta, Frayka, and Njall with angry shouts, as if they were somehow to blame.

"It's not our fault!" Greeta said, forgetting the Swamp Landers couldn't understand her. "We were trying to help!"

At the same time, two guards pulled Red Feather from the crowd and hauled him up the pyramid staircase.

"Red Feather!" Greeta shouted in panic. She realized too late that he wouldn't be able to hear her above the noisy crowds of the thousands still filling the city streets.

Several other guards appeared. They took Njall's dagger away from Greeta and gestured for Frayka to give them her dagger. Reluctantly, she did so. The guards then escorted Greeta, Frayka, and Njall away from the pyramid, through the city, and out of the city gate.

With the city of Xazaa erupting in turmoil behind them, the guards lit torches to guide their way through the oncoming night and led the Northlanders out into the jungle.

CHAPTER 19

Stunned by the sight of the smoke taking the shape of a dragon and attacking the king, Red Feather barely felt his feet touch the stone steps of the pyramid as he climbed them. He did, however, wince at the crushing strength of each guard pulling him up the staircase.

Looking up, Red Feather's heart sank at the sight at the top platform. Sitting on the platform, Jaya's body shook with heaving sobs while her two dragons kept a close and protective presence. One stood on its hind legs with its front paws pressed against Jaya's back, allowing the dragon to hover above her and monitor those around her. The creature hissed when Red Feather and the guards reached the platform.

The guards dragged Red Feather past

Jaya and her dragons toward the king's house where his family hovered and clung to each other at the front door. Compared to the king's finery, his wife and children wore colorful but less elaborate clothing. Their faces reflected the disturbance Red Feather felt.

A wide and simple wooden ladder leaned against the side of the home leading to its flat stone roof. The guards shoved Red Feather toward it. His mind raced as he tried to understand what they wanted from him.

The smoke dragon threw the king on top of the roof of his home. Do they think I can heal him?

Hopeful at that thought, Red Feather climbed up the ladder and onto the flat roof.

Fighting the sense that he trod on ground reserved for royalty, Red Feather took in his surroundings. He stepped over a low stone wall running along the edges of the rooftop. Stone pots lined the walls. Some contained water while others contained plants. Turning toward the center, he saw the king sprawled on his back and a kneeling man by his side, bent forward with his ear pressed against the king's chest.

Not knowing what else to do, Red Feather took several tentative steps toward them.

The kneeling man sat up but showed no surprise at Red Feather's presence. Black and white paint striped the kneeling man's body. A necklace of brightly colored feathers rested around his shoulders.

Red Feather assumed he must be a healer.

The healer spoke rapidly, but Red Feather understood nothing he said. The healer gestured for him to come closer.

Still feeling out of place, Red Feather approached the healer and king with caution until he became aware of the stillness of the king's body.

The ruler of Xazaa lay sprawled on his back. Although considered to be a tall man in the Great Turtle Lands, the king would likely stand only as high as the shoulders of Greeta and her Northlander friends. The white paint coating his skin had cracked, forming wayward lines across his body. His large nose reminded Red Feather of a hawk, despite the large dimple in the center of his chin.

Red Feather knelt opposite the healer and pressed his own ear against the king's chest, believing the urgency to save the king's life mattered more than decorum.

Red Feather heard no heart beat. He looked up at the healer, whose drawn face confirmed Red Feather's fear. To make the point clear, the healer gestured at the king's neck, which looked as limp as the broken neck of a rabbit caught for dinner.

The king is dead.

Stunned, Red Feather sat back on his heels. Forgetting the healer couldn't understand him, Red Feather said, "Then why did they bring me here? I can't save his life. I can't change what happened. What do you want from me?"

The healer nodded as if he somehow understood. He ran his fingers across a black stripe on his chest and said, "Kwah-tal." The healer then pointed at the stone wall surrounding them and down toward the plaza below. He raised his hand skyward, pointed at the king, and then pointed at the jungle behind them. Finally, he touched the black stripe on his chest again. "Kwah-tal."

"The smoke that took the shape of a dragon," Red Feather said. "Finehurst."

The healer spoke with an insistent tone. "Kwah-tal!"

"That is the name you call Finehurst," Red Feather said. "Kwah-tal."

The healer stood, walked around the king's body to Red Feather's side, and gestured for him to follow. The healer walked to a section of pots growing herbs and vegetables.

Confused, Red Feather joined his side. Thinking that the healer either understood some words of the Shining Star language or had the talent to detect Red Feather's intent, he said, "I don't understand. The king is dead. Nothing can bring him back to life. These herbs can do him no good."

The healer gestured toward the array of plants and said, "Kwah-tal." He pointed at the jungle again.

"These plants have something to do with Kwah-tal?" Red Feather said.

One of the plants shuddered at the mention of the name the Swamp Dragon healer used for Finehurst.

The healer brought his hands together in a soft clap and then pushed Red Feather closer to the plant that shuddered.

Baffled, Red Feather stared at it. A mass of rubbery green leaves stood on thick, pale pink stems. Looking closer, Red Feather saw how the leaves bore narrow red and white stripes. He saw no sign of fruit or vegetable. Nor did he see any evidence the plant might be an herb due to the size and sturdiness of its leaves.

Then what do they use this plant for? Why is it so important to the king?

Red Feather believed he'd more likely get answers from the plant itself than the healer. Moments ago, the plant shuddered when the others surrounding it remained still. And yet this plant appeared far sturdier and less likely to be moved by a gentle breeze than its neighbors. Red Feather strained to remember everything his uncle had ever mentioned about his travels and experiences with plants foreign to the Shining Star nation.

The last ray of light cast upon the platform disappeared with the setting sun. From high atop the pyramid, Red Feather looked up to see the city around him cast in twilight, which would soon fade to a deep, dark night.

Thousands of people still packed the avenues and streets. The air hummed with their worried conversations, and torches dotted the cityscape with light. The jungle beyond the city and its border of crops looked like a black abyss.

Finehurst is somewhere in that abyss.

Red Feather remembered that his uncle talked often of following his instincts. Uncle spoke about opening his heart and mind to the green spirits of the world and asking them to guide him.

But I have no idea how to do that. All I can do is guess.

Red Feather considered that all green life matters as much as mortal or animal life. He thought about his habit of treating all animals as equals. Right now, he stood high above the plant and remembered the times in his life when he felt threatened or belittled because others stood tall over him.

Red Feather sat directly across from the plant so that he felt on the same level with it. It seemed to him that opening his heart and mind in the hope of finding guidance would require silence and awareness. He lowered his gaze in reverence and focused his attention on listening even though he couldn't imagine how he might hear the guidance he needed.

For a long time, Red Feather sensed nothing. He kept his breath deep and even. He kept his focus on opening himself like a door to reveal an inviting space.

Perhaps he had expected to hear whispers or see images, but nothing like that happened. Instead, a certain type of knowing filled his thoughts. Red Feather waited patiently while the knowing poured through him like rain channeled through the city streets of Xazaa.

Following the new sense of knowledge that now pulsed in his veins, Red Feather looked up at the plant and extended his hands toward it. He touched its thick, rubbery leaves.

The leaves jerked away from his fingertips and curled inward.

I assumed too much too fast.

Red Feather placed his hands upon his chest and spoke to the plant. "I mean no disrespect or harm. I mean to ask for your help."

The plant quivered and kept its leaves curled up and tucked together.

"We are all in danger," Red Feather explained. "Based on everything I understand, I believe Finehurst has the power to harm all of the Great Turtle Lands. And possibly even more lands beyond our own."

The plant kept still.

Perhaps it only understands the Swamp Lander language.

Red Feather focused to remember the little he'd learned of that language. "Bad man. Finehurst. Must fight or he will hurt. Need help."

The plant remained still.

Of course. The plant has never heard the name Finehurst. What was it that the healer called him?

"Kwah-tal," Red Feather said. "Killed king. Dangerous. Need help."

Suddenly, all of the plant's leaves wrapped around Red Feather's hands and wrists with a powerful grip.

Startled, Red Feather tried to yank his hands free, but the leaves held on tight as if they planned to consume him.

CHAPTER 20

"I say we make a run for it," Njall said. He walked behind Greeta and ahead of Frayka on a narrow dirt path winding through the jungle and the black night.

"And go where?" Greeta said. In the dim light cast by the torches of the guards walking ahead, she gestured to the jungle.

It closed in so tightly around them that tree branches and undergrowth brushed against her skin with every step. More important, the clouded sky revealed no stars or moon. Without the guards and their torches, the jungle would go pitch black.

Knowing the guards didn't understand the Northlander language, Njall spoke freely. "Back where we came from."

A loud series of grunts sounded high in the canopy above. The dark and fierce noise made Greeta jump in surprise.

Moments later, other animals throughout the jungle answered with their own grunts.

"This place isn't like the Land of Ice," Greeta said. "There are wild animals here, and I wager they're far more dangerous than wild sheep."

Frayka spoke up from the back. "She's right. Remember those dragons that bit us? This place probably has all kinds of horrible creatures just waiting for us to make one wrong move so they can pounce and have us for supper."

As if in agreement, a low growl rumbled in the dark ahead.

"And they took our daggers!" Frayka complained. "How are we supposed to defend ourselves without weapons?"

Greeta felt Njall and Frayka cluster close behind while the guards in front of them shouted and waved their torches.

A large and sleek animal jumped onto the path in front of the guards. The size of a wolf, it laid its ears back flat and snarled.

The guards shouted louder and jabbed the flaming torches at the strange animal. It backed away and then disappeared into the jungle.

Greeta saw the fear and dismay on the faces of the guards in the torchlight. Seeing an opportunity, she seized it. Striding forward, she placed herself between the guards.

"We need our weapons," Greeta said. She looked at all the guards until she saw one with their daggers tucked under his belt. She pointed at the daggers and then at herself and the Northlanders standing behind.

The guards all spoke at once, gesturing for Greeta to back away.

"No!" Greeta said. She pointed at the path ahead where the animal had attacked. She then held out her empty hands. "What are we supposed to do if something like that happens again? What if you can't stop the next one? What if you get hurt or killed?"

Before the guards could disagree again, the one with their daggers gestured for the other guards to be silent. He spoke while mimicking Greeta's gesture of pointing at where the animal had intercepted them, at the other guards, and then at Greeta.

Another guard argued. He pointed at Greeta and the dagger. He then turned to another guard and acted as if he were stabbing him in the back with an invisible weapon.

Surprised, Greeta said to Frayka and Njall, "They think we want to ambush them."

"It's not a bad idea," Frayka said. "If we can get our daggers back, we should think about it."

"No!" Greeta protested. "No one is going to hurt these guards."

There was just enough light from the torches for Greeta to see Frayka and Njall exchange exasperated looks.

Turning back toward the guards, Greeta said, "No one will hurt you. I won't let them. All we want is to protect ourselves."

The guard who had spoken first studied Greeta. He gestured toward her and spoke to his colleagues. A few of them exchanged the same exasperated looks Greeta had seen pass between Frayka and Njall.

That means he's trying to convince them to give the daggers back to us. Why else would they look so pained?

With renewed hope, Greeta gave all her attention to the guard who appeared to agree with her. "We are strangers here," she said. "My friends are from the Land of Ice, and I'm from the Shining Star nation here in the Great Turtle Lands. But we know nothing of the Land of Swamp Dragons."

She gestured to the jungle surrounding them. "We don't know the dangers or how to protect ourselves. We need our weapons." Greeta placed a gentle hand on the guard's arm. "We need your help."

Another guard spoke angrily while he stepped between them and pushed Greeta away.

But the first guard's voice took on a reprimanding tone. The interfering guard looked down and stepped back.

The first guard spoke and placed an equally gentle hand on Greeta's shoulder.

Other guards protested and gestured toward the path ahead.

The first guard turned toward them and waved his hand at their torches.

The other guards hesitated and looked at each other. Finally, they murmured, seemingly in agreement at last.

"What is it?" Frayka said. "What's happening?"

"I don't know yet," Greeta said.

The first guard spoke to Greeta, seeming to explain their decision. He gestured to another guard, who handed his torch to Greeta.

Surprised, she accepted it.

When the first guard spoke again, he gave her the impression of asking a question.

Not knowing what else to do, Greeta nodded, hoping he would understand she meant to agree to whatever he suggested. She trusted it would be the right decision.

The first guard beckoned to the others, and two more guards handed their torches over to Frayka and Njall.

Taking the torch happily, Njall said, "I think we're getting somewhere."

The guards placed their hands on Njall's back and shoved him to the front until he stood ahead of everyone else.

Njall straightened himself. He took a nervous glance at the darkness ahead and then turned to look back at everyone standing behind him. "If they expect me to lead, the least they can do is hand over my dagger." He pointed at the first guard who still kept both daggers tucked under his belt.

As if understanding Njall's words, the first guard handed one of the daggers to Njall.

Njall accepted the weapon and examined it. "This isn't mine. It belongs to Frayka."

The guards pushed Greeta and Frayka to join Njall's side. The first guard passed the other dagger to the women.

Accepting it, Frayka gave the dagger a quick once-over. "You're right," Frayka said to Njall. "This one's yours."

Each holding a torch in one hand, they struggled at attempting to exchange daggers with no luck.

"Oh, here," Greeta said, extending her free hand with the palm open. "Each of you place the dagger you have on my hand and then pick up your own."

Following her suggestion, the Northlanders succeeded, now happy to have their own weapons back in hand.

The guards spoke and gestured for the Northlanders to continue.

"Gladly," Njall said to them. Grinning while he brandished his dagger, he said, "We'll show you why you should be happy to have the finest warriors in the world leading you through the jungle.

Loud grunts filled the treetops above them once again.

Njall flinched.

Greeta smiled and swept her free hand toward the dark path. "Lead on, noble Northland warrior."

To Njall's credit, he drew himself tall and forged ahead.

Greeta followed, hoping dawn would come soon.

After all, the guards had just placed Greeta and her friends in the dangerous position of leading the way toward the dark jungle and any monsters that might be waiting to attack.

CHAPTER 21

"Help!" Red Feather cried, panicked at the tight grip that the plant kept around his hand. All of its leaves enveloped his hand and wrist, which began to feel numb.

The healer knelt by Red Feather's side. Despite looking drawn and pale from the shock of finding the king's dead body here on the rooftop of the pyramid's uppermost platform, the healer shifted his focus to Red Feather and the plant that had attached itself to his hand. The healer removed his shirt and placed it on the stone floor between Red Feather and the pot that held the plant.

Standing, the healer gestured for Red Feather to do the same.

"You don't understand," Red Feather said, feeling more frantic because he could no longer feel his own hand. "It won't let go!"

The healer placed a calming hand on Red Feather's shoulder. He spoke words in the Swamp Lander language that Red Feather didn't understand.

A sense of tranquility eased Red Feather's shoulders. He remembered that just moments ago he'd felt even more serene when a sense of knowing rained through him. It made him feel confident and at peace. Perhaps it still existed inside him, standing in the shadow of his fright.

This isn't the time to doubt. Surely, this healer understands the plant and what it's doing. I have to trust him.

Red Feather looked up at the healer and nodded his understanding of what the man wanted him to do. Red Feather shifted his body until he could find a kneeling position and then stood up. All the time, he kept a close eye on the plant and used his free hand to hold onto the stone pot for balance.

The healer leaned forward and plunged his hands into the pot. He dug his hands around all of the pot's edges and loosened the dirt. With great effort, he lifted the plant out of the pot and put it on the shirt he'd placed on the stone floor. He then tied the shirt around the plant's ball of roots to keep the dirt around them.

The plant relaxed and let go of Red Feather's hand. Its leaves returned to their previous position.

Red Feather shook his hand until all the feeling returned to it. Knowing neither the healer nor the plant could understand him, Red Feather spoke anyway. "I don't understand. What does this mean?"

Without any sign that he understood or even acknowledged the question, the healer picked up the bound plant and shoved it into Red Feather's arms. The healer then led Red Feather back to the ladder at the edge of the rooftop.

Red Feather shifted the plant in his arms until he discovered he could hold it in the crook of one elbow, which allowed him to keep one hand free. Following the healer's urging, Red Feather climbed onto the ladder and descended, still holding the plant in the crook of his arm.

When he reached the surface of the top platform, Red Feather found himself alone. He looked up for guidance.

The healer remained on the rooftop but gestured for Red Feather to enter the king's home.

"I can't," Red Feather said. "I don't know much about your people, but I know enough to understand that I'm not allowed in the home of royalty."

The healer's gestures became more insistent.

Red Feather looked down the long stone

staircase leading to the city below. The thousands of citizens who had come to witness the ceremony of the serpent shadow descending the pyramid still crowded every street and avenue. The number of torches had grown, and the city now stood awash in glowing light.

Someone in the crowd below pointed at Red Feather and shouted. Others followed suit, and a few people shook their fists in his direction.

Maybe it's safer to do what the healer wants.

The plant rustled against his arm as if impatient for Red Feather to make a decision.

I'm supposed to deliver the plant to the royal family. That must be why the healer keeps pointing toward their home.

Better to face the wrath of the guards to the king's home than the restless crowd below. Red Feather walked toward the open doorway of the small and square stone house. Although the king's family had emerged during Finehurst's attack, they'd disappeared. Most likely, back into their home.

Guards flanked the simple entrance. They bristled until one pointed out the plant Red Feather held in the crook of one arm to his comrade. The guards entered a heated debate. After a few minutes, a woman's voice called out from inside the king's home.

Jaya emerged with the two swamp dragons at her heels. The paint covering her face was ruined by streaks of tears. She caught her breath at the sight of the plant. Jaya spoke to the guards, who fell quiet and resumed their stations by the door. Gesturing for Red Feather to follow, she went back into the king's home.

Overwhelmed by nerves, Red Feather stood in place and chattered in his own Shining Star language, even though he knew Jaya would understand little of what he said. "I don't believe it's my place to be in the royal home. Your king is dead. Everyone needs time to grieve, especially his family. I suppose you work for them or have some special type of duty that involves your dragons, but I don't."

The guards exchanged startled looks at his reluctance to move, and one of them gestured frantically for Red Feather to enter the king's home.

The leaves of the plant in his arms strained toward the entrance as if reaching out to it.

"Fine," Red Feather muttered.

A few steps later he walked through the entrance and found the inside of the home to be more stark and plain than its exterior. Other than Jaya and her dragons, he saw no one else inside. The space stood empty of any type of furniture or rug. It looked like an unused storage space.

But when he followed Jaya to the opposite end, Red Feather discovered a square opening in the floor that revealed a stone staircase leading to the interior of the pyramid.

The two swamp dragons plopped down and curled around the opening. One yawned and then rested its jaw on its folded paws. The other snapped at a cloud of dust.

Still clutching the plant, Red Feather followed Jaya down the stairs and stared at the wonders below. Small torches hung on the inwardly sloping walls and cast a soft light throughout a room larger than the false home above. The white paint on the walls made the space appear bright and spacious. Arrangements of tall and brightly colored feathers gave a sense of luxury. Several quiet and somber people sat on elegantly carved stone benches by a collection of tables that created square and triangular patterns throughout the space.

Red Feather reached the bottom of the staircase and paused when he recognized the seated people as the royal family. None seemed to notice his presence, so he continued walking behind Jaya. She wove among the maze of tables to a far corner where an especially large table presented a strange sight: tiny jungles, crops, and cities covered the tabletop.

Jaya stood at one end of the table and gestured for Red Feather to join her side.

Once he'd done so, Jaya swept her arms across the table and spoke.

Red Feather had learned enough of Jaya's language to know she'd referred to the tiny landscape as the Land of Swamp Dragons.

Jaya pointed to the city in the center of the tabletop and said, "Xazaa."

Red Feather would have recognized it without her help. Located in the city's center, a model of the pyramid in which they now stood looked small enough to fit in the palm of his hand. A painted clay doll of the king stood atop the pyramid model. Red Feather knew all of the streets surrounding it, as well as the marketplace and all the other buildings of Xazaa.

Jaya pointed at several other cities spread throughout the nation and named each one. Each city had its own central pyramid with the doll of a king standing on top. Jaya spoke again, but Red Feather understood nothing she said. Jaya picked up the doll of a king from a nearby city and used it to knock off the doll of the king of Xazaa.

Red Feather frowned. Did Jaya think another king in the Land of Swamp Dragons had taken the form of smoke to kill the king?

Seeming to note his confusion, Jaya leaned toward a corner of the table and picked up the ruler of a different city. She placed the king of Xazaa back atop his pyramid and used the other doll to knock him off.

War, Red Feather realized with a start. *She's telling me the king's death will start a war.*

Before Shadow had disappeared, she told Red Feather about the unique way in which the people of the Land of Swamp Dragons kept peace. Royalty ruled their cities like independent kingdoms, but all cities stood united as a nation. One city could wage war against another at any time, but only the rulers would fight. The triumphant king allowed the defeated one to remain in charge, but the conquered city must consider itself to be indebted to the champion.

Shadow believed Xazaa had defeated all cities in the Land of Swamp Dragons and that its king was the greatest champion in its history.

What will happen now that he's dead?

Red Feather didn't understand why Jaya had brought him here or the purpose of the plant he held. But he realized she had just told him that the city of Xazaa would likely come under attack as soon as word spread of its king's death.

A new king should protect the city. But

who is the new king?

Emboldened by the way Jaya seemed to place her confidence in him, Red Feather picked up the fallen doll of the king of Xazaa. Placing the doll flat on its back in the palm of his hand, Red Feather spoke, hoping Jaya would understand the intent of his question even though she might not understand his mix of Shining Star and Swamp Lander words. "Who is the new king?"

Jaya's lower lip trembled for a brief moment until she pressed her lips together to make the trembling stop. She took the tiny doll from Red Feather's hand and looked at it for several long moments. Holding onto the doll, she gestured for Red Feather to follow her again.

Returning to the area by the stairway, Red Feather averted his eyes from the weeping members of the king's family. He didn't want to intrude upon their grief or inadvertently do anything that might cause them more. When Jaya walked into the group, he stayed close to her, hoping he might somehow be less conspicuous.

However, Jaya spoke loudly and pointed at Red Feather and the plant he held.

The king's family stared long and hard at Red Feather. Mortified, he wished he could disappear. But then a new thought struck him.

Who is Jaya to speak to the king's family

like this? Was she his advisor?

Red Feather realized that while he had easily recognized the roles of many people in the city, such as merchants and guards, he never understood Jaya's place in Xazaa. He'd assumed she acted as some sort of scout because she spent so much time outside the city, always accompanied by her dragons.

A man old enough to be the king's brother took a step forward and argued.

Red Feather recognized a few words but not enough to know what the argument was about.

Jaya held the doll of the king between her forefinger and thumb, extending it forward for all to see. When she spoke, her voice quivered and yet sounded strong.

The king's brother lowered his gaze and stepped back.

Jaya spoke with intent and purpose. She held her free hand toward the plant, and its leaves reached out to touch her skin. Nodding acknowledgement to the plant, she moved her hand to grip Red Feather's shoulder.

Red Feather steadied himself and looked at the royal family standing before him while Jaya talked. Her grip on his shoulder felt strong but frightened him.

Is she reminding them that other cities will attack? Is Jaya afraid because the king won't be able to protect them?

Red Feather remembered how Jaya, despite the cool distance of her nature, had been kind to him from the first day he'd arrived in Xazaa. She'd been the one to recognize his affinity with plants and made it possible for him to earn his place in the city, even though he always assumed it would only last until Shadow returned. There had been times when Jaya appeared to argue on his behalf with others. Red Feather often suspected she protected him.

He drew himself up tall. Jaya acted like a good friend, and now he wanted to return her kindness by standing at her side when she seemed to need an ally and possibly even a friend.

Still speaking, Jaya took his free hand and led Red Feather through the gathering of the king's family members until they reached a large stone chair raised upon a platform. Jaya positioned him by the side of the stone chair.

She then stood in front of the large chair while the king's family gathered before her. Without another word, Jaya turned her back on them and climbed onto the platform. Turning to face them again, she sat in the chair.

The king's family knelt before her.

Surprised, Red Feather turned to look at Jaya. Now seeing her profile, he stared at her hawk-like nose and the large dimple in the center of her chin.

Jaya isn't a scout or messenger for the king, Red Feather realized with a start. *She's his daughter. His eldest child.*

Taking another look at her kneeling family, Red Feather understood.

And now she's king of Xazaa.

CHAPTER 22

By the time the sun peeked over the tree line of the jungle, Greeta, Frayka, Njall, and the guards trailing behind them arrived at a wide gate made of gigantic curving bones, each one larger than the height of any mortal. Bleached by years of exposure to the sun, the bones now picked up the rosy color of the new daylight.

Greeta shivered at the horrible sight. "Are those real bones? What kinds of monsters live in the jungle?"

Njall and Frayka laughed. Njall stepped forward and ran his hand across one bone. "These are the ribs of whales."

Confused, Greeta turned toward Frayka for an explanation.

"Whales," Frayka stated plainly. "They live in the sea." She held her arms wide apart. "Big things. Like giants swimming next to ships." Puzzled, she said, "You never saw one?"

Greeta shook her head.

"Maybe they don't have them where she lives," Njall said, still admiring the gate.

"But they have them here." Frayka brightened. "Maybe this is where they disappear to in the winter!" Turning to Greeta, she added, "We see whales only part of the year. We think the winter seas get too cold for them to tolerate."

The guards trailing behind caught up with the Northlanders at the whale-bone gate and then yelled to those standing watch on the other side. Moments later, the gates swung open, and the guards herded the Northlanders inside.

The Xazaa guards talked heatedly with the guards of the gate.

At the same time, Greeta took in her new surroundings. Instead of the uneven dirt path they'd followed through the jungle, she now stood on an avenue paved with wide, flat stones. Even though the jungle pressed against the edges of the avenue and formed a canopy overhead, it formed a space wide enough for several people to walk side by side.

Expecting to see the avenue open up into another city like Xazaa, Greeta was surprised to see it lead to another whale-bone gate far ahead.

The Xazaa guards escorted the North-

landers along the avenue until they reached the next gate. Again, the Xazaa guards
convinced the guards at the second gate to
open it, and then repeated their previous
conversation.

Once the second gate opened and allowed the Xazaa guards and Northlanders to
enter, Greeta saw that the paved avenue
continued toward yet another large gate
made of carved stone. Even from a distance, she could tell that the carvings were
similar to the ones she'd seen on the
buildings in Xazaa.

"What is this place?" Frayka said. She
paced, gazing from one gate to the next.
"And why are there so many gates?"

"Don't know," Njall said. "The only reason to have gates is to protect something
you treasure." He gestured toward the Xazaa guards who had led them through the
jungle. "But it seems they're having a
harder time making their case."

Greeta followed his gaze to the group of
guards deep in discussion. "Our guards?"

Njall nodded. "Second gate didn't take
as long as the first gate. But the third
gate's taking the longest. Wonder why."

The night had left a chill in the air.
Noticing it for the first time, Greeta shivered. "Does anyone else feel like we're walking into the heart of someplace where we
don't belong?"

Frayka sighed. "Since the moment our

ship landed in this horrible country."

"I'm not talking about the Land of Swamp Dragons," Greeta said. "I mean this specific place. It's not like Xazaa or the beach where we landed or the river we followed."

Njall shuddered. "At least the trees don't try to eat people here." He paused and looked all around. "Not yet."

"What if Finehurst is here?" Greeta said. "Or close by?"

"Finehurst?" Frayka said. "Why do you think they have anything to do with Finehurst?"

"I think the smoke dragon came in this direction," Greeta said. "Maybe even to this place."

"Smoke dragon." Frayka snorted. "That was just some trick."

"No trick," Njall said. "It's the same smoke dragon that gave me to the tree for breakfast. Maybe it's Finehurst himself. Maybe it's some magic he's worked."

Greeta paced. "It seems like the smoke dragon was headed in this direction when we saw it go into the jungle."

Frayka's voice took a deeper and more serious tone. "Is there something you're not telling us?"

The question reminded Greeta of the consideration of the next seven generations practiced by the Shining Star people because she'd failed to think of it when she'd faced Finehurst's image on the beach.

Even worse, Greeta had failed to be completely truthful with her Northlander friends about her experience before they arrived on the beach. Without knowing the truth, how could they be aware of the extent of danger they faced? "I tried to tell you about the smoke we first saw after landing, but I never told you everything that happened before you came ashore."

"Ashore?" Njall said, his face scrunching up in confusion. "What shore?"

"The shore we found when we came to the Land of Swamp Dragons," Greeta said. "The shore we found when we followed Finehurst across the sea from the Land of Ice."

Frayka crossed her arms but nestled against Njall's chest as if declaring her allegiance and preparing to take sides if need be. "That's right. Njall and I were thrown into the sea off shore. When we walked onto the beach, you were already there."

Njall tightened his grip on Frayka's shoulder. "Finehurst's ship was gone. But you knew where to find it."

"Greeta said she saw Finehurst on his ship before it sailed through the air into the jungle." Frayka spoke to Njall but kept a close eye on Greeta. "We know it wasn't Finehurst but an image of him instead.

Because of what the dead men told us." Frayka's expression hardened. "What exactly did you see, Greeta?"

Greeta glanced at the guards with the hope they might interrupt and guide them through the next gate. But the guards argued with each other and ignored the Northlanders.

The pain Greeta felt when she'd been betrayed by her sweetheart and cousin dug deep into her chest. She'd found a new sense of home with Frayka and Njall, but now the truth she'd failed to tell them threatened to tear them apart.

What's wrong with me? Why can't I keep the people I care about close to me?

With a sinking sense of sadness, Greeta decided the time had come to tell them the truth she should have shared when it first happened. "When Finehurst's ship landed on the beach, I didn't know where you were or if you were still alive. He turned to step through his sail, and that's when I saw he looked like a reflection on a sheet of ice. I'd wondered about all the strange things he'd done. I accused Finehurst's reflection of acting like a guard to keep Norah imprisoned at the ice castle, and it acted as if I'd uncovered the truth."

Frayka's stare grew with intensity. "Did you accuse him of anything else?"

"I asked him why he'd done those strange things. Why he made a ship of ice and left the castle. Why he took Njall but left the Northlander ship behind for us. Why he led us to Tower Island and then here to the Great Turtle Lands." Greeta shrugged. "He didn't answer."

"But you know the answer," Njall said, pointing at Greeta. "I can see it in your eyes."

"I think he used us to get the tapestry pieces he's missing," Greeta said. "I don't think Finehurst was in the Land of Ice. But that magic image that he made of himself manipulated us. Maybe Finehurst is here or maybe it's only his image that's here. I think he's going to try to steal the final tapestry pieces from us."

"And once he has a complete tapestry, he'll have the power to control or kill whoever he wants," Njall said.

The Northlanders looked at each other, and Greeta imagined they all had the same thought.

We hid the tapestry pieces on our ship. And Finehurst doesn't seem to know that. If Finehurst had what he wanted, he would have no reason to follow us.

In that moment, Greeta realized she needed to tell her companions everything for their own protection. "When Finehurst's ship began to leave, I threw a rock at his image and shattered it. The pieces fell onto the beach. I used another rock to smash each piece into shards, and black smoke came out of them." Greeta steadied herself. "Everything that the smoke dragon has done is my fault. I'm the one who released it. If I hadn't smashed those ice shards, it might still be trapped inside them."

"The smoke dragon," Njall whispered.

Greeta nodded. "All the smoke attached to Finehurst's ship, and it flew in the air and toward the jungle. The ice that I broke into shards melted by the time I saw you."

Frayka nodded her understanding. "I say we follow the smoke. I think you're right. It might be here or close by."

The guards walked away from their own conversation and escorted the Northlanders through the gates that now swung open.

CHAPTER 23

While the surviving family of the king of Xazaa mourned through the night of his death, Jaya took Red Feather down another staircase leading to a deeper level inside the pyramid. She gestured for him to leave the plant he'd removed from the building's highest platform on the bottom step.

With torch in hand, Jaya walked to the center of the large space and lit a circle of standing torches. Their light spread like sunshine throughout the deeper level and illuminated its brightly painted walls.

Red Feather stared at the walls surrounding him, each divided into horizontal strips that framed a series of images of people, animals, and monsters.

These are stories.

Overwhelmed by the many images all

around him, Red Feather wondered if they represented stories of the history of the Land of Swamp Dragons or their gods or their wishes.

Jaya spoke his name and gestured for Red Feather to join her where two walls met. He followed the direction of her finger, which pointed at the highest row of images on the wall to their right. Jaya spoke slowly, and Red Feather recognized a few words: rain, sun, corn.

The first image showed a monstrous figure bedecked in a cloak of bright blue feathers. Red Feather realized he beheld the image of the rain god, not a monster. He'd heard many of the merchants talk about this god in recent days because the crops needed rain. But Red Feather had little more than a vague understanding of this god's purpose and relationship to the Swamp Landers.

Jaya continued speaking, but she became so animated that Red Feather found it more difficult to make out anything she said. However, the images she pointed out told a story that he understood.

On the wall paintings, the rain god appeared to greet the king of Xazaa. The rain god pointed at another winged god hovering in the sky. Dark clouds and bolts of lightning surrounded the winged god.

Jaya pointed at the winged god and clapped her hands together while making a booming noise.

"I see," Red Feather said. He pointed from one image to another. "There is a rain god but there is also a god of thunder and lightning. And I believe they work together." To illustrate his point, Red Feather took Jaya's hands in his and clasped them as he would grip a friend's hands.

Jaya gave him a brief and startled look, which reminded Red Feather that she now acted as king and probably expected to be treated like royalty. "Apologies," Red Feather said, hearing the distress in his voice.

But when he tried to pull his hands free, Jaya held on with a firm grip and smiled. She said a single word that Red Feather believed had something to do with being allies. He nodded his understanding, and Jaya then released his hands.

The next image showed the king walking inside the pyramid in which Red Feather now stood with Jaya. He winced at the images showing the king sticking a barb into his tongue and drawing blood.

Noticing Red Feather's further distress, Jaya spoke to him in a soothing voice. She pointed from the image of the king drawing blood from himself to the images that followed, which illustrated the stars in the night sky, the moon, and the sun. Jaya pointed to the following image showing Xazaa surrounded by bountiful crops.

Red Feather studied the images. "Jaya."

She looked at him.

Red Feather shook his head in sorrow. "You're going to hurt yourself to appease the gods and keep the world balanced? Is that what this means?"

Jaya resumed her narrative and pointed to another row of images that continued to show the king drawing blood from himself. A large serpent appeared, and it resembled the shadow of the serpent that had seemed to crawl down the pyramid at sunset. The king showed no fear of the serpent. In the following images, a warrior crawled out of the serpent's mouth.

That warrior carried the same plant that Red Feather had brought inside the pyramid. He recognized its shape and color. In the image, the plant pointed its leaves at the king.

Jaya paused to smile at Red Feather.

"That can't mean me." Red Feather swallowed hard. "I have never been much of a warrior. I'm better at sensing trouble before it happens. In the Shining Star nation, we prevent wars. We hardly ever fight them."

Jaya patted him on the back as if Red Feather had just promised to fight to the death for her. She led him to the adjacent wall and pointed to a new series of images that showed the journey of the warrior that had emerged from the serpent's mouth.

The king placed drops of his blood on the surface of the leaves, which absorbed it. The images showed the warrior traveling through the jungle with the plant and fighting off terrifying animals. Finally, the warrior arrived at a gate and entered a small city at the foot of a pyramid. Each block of stone that formed the base of the pyramid bore the image of a dragon.

Next, a great dragon made of smoke appeared on the steps of the pyramid to block the way of the warrior.

A sense of dread ran through Red Feather. He turned to look at Jaya only to be dismayed at the sight of the same dread he felt reflected in her eyes.

* * *

After searching Red Feather's eyes for a moment, Jaya breathed in new strength.

She liked the Shining Star man. She admired the way he'd tried to help fight the smoke dragon when all others had stood by and done nothing. Her fellow Swamp Landers had been too afraid to act. Or they'd assumed approaching the royal pyramid would result in punishment. Only this Shining Star man had tried to help Jaya and her father.

Red Feather understood only a little of her language, but Jaya knew she had no time to waste. She had to hope he would understand enough.

"I always assumed these portents were about a Swamp Lander man, but you're the only one who stepped forward." Jaya glanced at the walls surrounding her, frustrated that there were no pictures to help her explain. "Long ago, our gods agreed to help the gods of another land because they said all gods are brothers and sisters. That is the most important thing to understand. Everything here is about that agreement. And now you've become part of that agreement."

Jaya pointed at the image that showed the warrior raising the plant high above his head while opening his mouth. She pointed at the warrior's open mouth and then at Red Feather. She spoke a short phrase in the Swamp Lander language, careful to enunciate each word with precision. "Et vuu sway." *We stand united.* Jaya repeated the phrase and then pointed to Red Feather.

His face lit up with understanding, but then Red Feather shook his head in protest. He pointed at the warrior in the image on the wall. When he spoke in the Shining Star language, Jaya understood enough to know he doubted himself.

Jaya faced him with patience and determination. She repeated the phrase twice more. "Et vuu sway. Et vuu sway!"

Red Feather shook his head in dismay but then focused on the words Jaya said

and repeated them until he could pro-
nounce them to her satisfaction. "Uht vuu
sway."

"Good," Jaya said. "This next part
shows what you must do, but it is not
enough to defeat the smoke dragon. You
will need help from another warrior."

Jaya pointed at the next images: the
leaves of the plant attacked the smoke
dragon. Those leaves flew through the air
like arrows and impaled the creature. The
smoke dragon collapsed onto the ground
and formed a black trail. The warrior stepped across the trail and continued up the
pyramid steps where he met the king of
Xazaa again. The king led the warrior
along the black trail that had once been
the smoke dragon into the ground beneath
the pyramid and the city where they met
and defeated monsters. Finally, they
climbed above ground and entered a temple.

When Red Feather looked at the last
image, Jaya watched the shock register on
his face. He stood as still as if he'd seen a
ghost.

The last image showed a tapestry hanging on the temple wall and a woman
standing in front of it. In the picture, that
woman stood tall with pale skin and long
blonde hair.

"It's Greeta," Jaya said. "Her gods are
the ones that our gods promised to help.

We know she is the warrior who must help you defeat the smoke dragon, but the details of how the gods said she will help you were lost long ago."

CHAPTER 24

When the guards escorted them through the third gate, the small size of the city they encountered surprised Greeta. Like Xazaa, its stone buildings were painted blood red and surrounded by avenues and a plaza.

Unlike Xazaa, the city consisted of a square temple in front of a flat-top pyramid like the one in Xazaa but smaller. While Xazaa's population consisted of thousands, Greeta imagined fewer than 100 people lived in this city, although she imagined its population must have been larger in the past.

A high stone wall surrounded the city and separated it from the crops and jungle outside. Greeta nudged Frayka and gestured toward the wall. "Why do you think they have that?"

"They're keeping something out," Fray-ka said. "Or keeping something in."

"Might be for protection from those animals that attacked us," Njall chimed in.

"Look how empty the streets are," Greeta said. "It isn't a city like Xazaa. What if this is part of Xazaa? Wouldn't that explain why the city guards let us in? What if this little city is protecting something that belongs to Xazaa?"

The guards signaled for them to walk into the city.

The temple's large wooden door swung open, and a group of women wearing simple sheath dresses over their painted skin emerged. They approached with quick strides.

A woman wearing bright yellow paint with black zigzag designs gave the impression of being in charge. She pointed at Greeta and yelled at the guards who had escorted her from Xazaa.

"This is bad." Frayka tensed. "Njall, be ready."

With a start, Greeta understood what Frayka meant. When the guards allowed the Northlanders to lead the way through the jungle last night, they'd returned the daggers that belonged to Frayka and Njall. But when they arrived at this city, the guards forgot to take them back.

"Wait," Greeta said. "We don't know what they want. And your dragon bites are still healing." Glancing at her friends, she saw bloodstains on their bandages.

The Xazaa guards argued with the yellow-painted woman.

The other women, painted blue and brown and red, kept a close eye on the Northlanders but stayed a good distance away from them.

Frayka and Njall tensed. They split their attention between the Xazaa guards and the brightly painted women. "We know these guards were told to bring us here," Frayka said. "And I suspect we are not welcome."

"Or possibly too welcome," Njall said.

Confused, Greeta said, "What does that mean?"

The woman with bright yellow skin jabbed her finger at the guards. She then waved her hands at the Northlanders as if their presence meant trouble.

"He means they're blaming us for the king's death," Frayka said. "And these people will make sure we pay for it."

Frayka's words hit Greeta like a punch in the gut. She panicked at the thought of being separated from her friends.

We followed Finehurst's image here to the Land of Swamp Dragons. But did his smoke dragon somehow lead us to Xazaa, or did we lead it there?

"What if we had something to do with the king's death?" Greeta said.

Frayka gave her a sharp look. "We bear no responsibility for that. What is wrong with you?"

Unconvinced, Greeta kept her worries to herself.

The argument between the yellow-painted woman and the Xazaa guards escalated. They talked over each other in voices that became louder by the moment and drew the attention of the other painted women.

"Now!" Frayka whispered.

Frayka and Njall drew their daggers and backed toward the gate through which they'd just passed.

"We will be leaving now," Frayka announced, even though only the other Northlanders could understand her words.

The Xazaa guards and the painted woman stopped arguing and turned to stare at the Northlanders.

"Greeta, come with us," Njall said.

Greeta stood her ground. "And go where?"

"Back to our ship," Frayka said. She glanced behind to make sure none of the guards who were now on the other side of the gate saw her approach. "We can stop at Xazaa and pick up that Shining Star little man you like so much."

"Red Feather," Greeta said, noticing how her heart thumped when she said his name.

Instead of deciding with her thoughts, Greeta decided with her instinct. She darted toward Njall and Frayka.

The yellow-painted woman ran in front of Greeta, intercepting her path before she could reach the other Northlanders. The Swamp Lander woman clamped her hand around Greeta's wrist and yelled at the guards. Although Greeta towered over the yellow-painted woman, the Swamp Lander's strength matched hers.

Unable to break free, Greeta shouted, "Run! Find Red Feather!"

The yellow-painted woman shouted, still clinging to Greeta.

In response, the other women surrounded Greeta. Within moments, Greeta found herself face-down in the dirt with her hands tied behind her back.

At the same time, the gate behind Frayka and Njall opened. The guards behind that gate joined the Xazaa guards when they rushed at the Northlanders. The local guards approached from behind and aimed their bodies at the Northlanders' knees to make them buckle.

Caught by surprise, Njall and Frayka toppled backwards and fell on top of their attackers.

The Xazaa guards then moved in swiftly to wrench away their daggers.

The painted women helped Greeta sit up in time to see her companions bound and gagged.

In that moment, Greeta's heart sank, and she felt like a fool.

They were right. I should have listened to Frayka and Njall from the day we arrived in the Land of Swamp Dragons. We don't know these people. We don't know what they're capable of doing to foreigners like us.

We never should have trusted them.

The yellow-painted woman left Greeta's side and walked to a point midway between the captured Northlanders.

Greeta paid close attention. Even though she understood very little of the Swamp Lander language, she believed she might be able to read the intent behind the words.

The yellow-painted woman ignored the Northlanders and gave her full attention to all the guards. Gesturing with her hands, she appeared to be explaining something.

One of the Xazaa guards asked a question, and his friends nodded their interest in learning the answer.

The yellow-painted woman turned to face Greeta but looked past her. The Swamp Lander woman pointed beyond Greeta at the temple behind her. She answered more questions while still gesturing toward the temple.

Before turning away, the yellow-painted woman looked into Greeta's eyes and pointed from Greeta to the temple.

They plan to take me into the temple.

The yellow-painted woman followed the guards toward Frayka and Njall, who struggled to free themselves. They yelled behind the gags, but Greeta couldn't understand them.

The guards talked at length, seeming to consider multiple options. While they spoke, the yellow-painted woman looked at the ground and shook her head repeatedly.

She doesn't like whatever the guards are saying.

Finally, the yellow-painted woman interrupted the guards and spoke rapidly and with conviction. She pointed at a small stone house at the opposite end of the city.

A Xazaa guard asked a brief question, and the yellow-painted woman nodded her response.

The local guards and Xazaa guards spoke to each other, seeming to come to an agreement.

The Xazaa guards hauled Frayka and Njall to their feet and then led them into the city.

They're separating us!

But why? What are they going to do with us?

Confident that none of the Swamp Landers could understand the Northlander language, Greeta shouted at Frayka and Njall. "If you can get free and escape, leave me here and save yourselves! Find Red Feather! He can help!"

Frayka kicked, while Njall lunged from side to side in an attempt to break loose.

The guards knocked them to the ground and kept them pinned. Within minutes, the painted women brought long strips of cloth, which the guards wrapped around Frayka and Njall to add another layer of binding.

Greeta stared in horror. Each of her companions looked like a gigantic cocoon with a butterfly imprisoned.

The guards dragged Frayka and Njall into the city.

Grief overwhelmed Greeta.

Why didn't I listen to Frayka? She told me not to trust any of the Swamp Landers from the very beginning. She warned me. If I'd paid attention to her good sense instead of mine, none of this would have happened!

A new idea struck Greeta: maybe it wasn't too late.

The yellow-painted woman gave instructions to her colleagues, who then escorted Greeta toward the temple where they appeared to live.

Greeta put up no resistance. Instead, she pretended to be stunned by the turn of events. She then pretended to follow them willingly.

For a moment, Greeta thought about the Shining Star nation and what she'd learned from them throughout the course of her life: to think through every decision and how it might impact the next seven generations.

But Greeta didn't care about the next seven generations. At this moment, she only cared about Frayka and Njall. She would escape and help them.

And if that meant she would have to hurt or kill someone, then so be it.

I'll look for the best opportunity. Before we reach the temple, I'll break free.

And then I will run.

CHAPTER 25

Standing inside the pyramid next to Jaya, Red Feather stared in disbelief at the last image in a series of wall paintings: an image of Greeta standing in front of a tapestry.

Even if the image didn't bear such a striking resemblance to her, Red Feather would have recognized her because Jaya had pointed at the image and spoken Greeta's name.

He still reeled from everything he'd gleaned from Jaya. The images showed a warrior emerging from the mouth of the serpent whose shadow had crawled down the pyramid several hours ago, and Jaya indicated Red Feather must be that warrior. He'd learned a phrase from her to speak to Finehurst's smoke dragon, which had destroyed the serpent shadow and murdered the king. Although not quite sure how things would work, Red Feather believed the words he spoke would allow the plant he'd befriended to attack and destroy the smoke dragon.

And then it seemed Red Feather must make some kind of journey where he would fight monsters but then climb above ground into a new city where he'd find Greeta.

Red Feather didn't relish the idea of fighting monsters. He'd much rather spend his time among plants and use them to heal. But he needed to find Greeta and take her back to their Shining Star village.

If I have to fight monsters to find Greeta, then I will fight monsters.

But how and where do I begin?

Red Feather backtracked to the earlier images Jaya had pointed out to him. He gestured toward the one showing the warrior traveling through the jungle. "If I take this journey, how do I know where to go?"

He stepped back and searched for another image. Finding it, he pointed at the image showing the warrior's first destination: a city with a temple. "This isn't Xazaa. What city is this? How do I find it?" Red Feather opened his arms to all the walls bearing images. "I know little about the Land of Swamp Dragons, much less where Finehurst's smoke dragon will go next."

Jaya walked away from the walls bearing the images. She pointed at the plant he'd left on the step and then ascended the stairs.

Red Feather hurried to catch up and picked up the plant while keeping Jaya in sight. He followed her back to the floor where her relatives grieved and to the table that displayed a miniature version of the Land of Swamp Dragons.

Jaya pointed at the largest city on the table. "Xazaa."

"Fine," Red Feather said. "We are here."

She called out to one of the dragons.

Red Feather heard the scrape of claws against stone and then the uncertain patter of large paws navigating the trek down the stairs from outside the pyramid. Several moments later, one of the dragons plopped at her feet.

Jaya spoke to the dragon until she coaxed the animal back on its feet. She then commanded it until the dragon reluctantly hauled itself up on its hind legs and placed its front paws on the edge of the table to lean against it. The dragon now stood slightly taller than its master.

Jaya took Red Feather's hands and cupped them facing down above the model of the Xazaa pyramid. She commanded the dragon again and slapped its back.

The dragon shook its head and grimaceed as if it tasted something awful.

Jaya gave its back an especially hard smack.

The dragon coughed up a mouthful of black smoke, which Jaya waved toward the tiny pyramid under Red Feather's hands.

Despite a sudden rush of nervousness, Red Feather remembered something he'd seen hours ago when the smoke dragon attacked.

The dragons snapped at it. They must have swallowed some of the smoke!

When the puff of black smoke drifted toward the tiny pyramid, Red Feather used one hand to keep it around the building, still holding the plant with his other hand. When the smoke attempted to rise, he pushed it back down.

Jaya touched his hands and pulled them away.

The smoke swirled around the miniature pyramid and took the shape of a dragon.

Jaya plucked a leaf from the plant in Red Feather's arms.

The plant shuddered and then nestled against Red Feather's chest.

Jaya stabbed the tiny smoke dragon with the leaf.

The smoke became denser, impaled by the leaf. The smoke dragon ran up to the top of the miniature pyramid and jumped

RESA NELSON

from its highest platform. Launching itself over the model city of Xazaa, the smoke dragon burst apart in mid-air and fell into the small jungle surrounding it.

Excited, Jaya leaned over the table bearing the expansive model of the Land of Swamp Dragons. She gestured for Red Feather to follow her lead.

Shifting the plant to cradle in the crook of one arm, Red Feather leaned forward. The black remains of the tiny smoke dragon now formed a winding path through the jungle. The path headed west and ended at a small city made up of a temple and a pyramid surrounded by gates and a high wall. Homes similar to the ones on the outskirts of Xazaa nestled outside the wall.

That's just like what the picture showed, except in miniature. We just killed a version of the smoke dragon, and its remains have created a new path.

Red Feather pointed along the path and then at the final destination of the small city and its temple. "This is where you want me to go."

Once more, Jaya motioned for him to follow her. They climbed the stairs leading outside to the enclosed entrance. At the top of the stairs, the dragon that had stayed behind to guard the entrance curled up and dozed. When Jaya spoke to it, the dragon blinked sleepily and then lumbered to its feet. Moments later, the other dragon clambered up the stairs to join its comrade.

Red Feather walked with Jaya through the dark entrance with the dragons close on their heels.

When they neared the open doorway, Jaya spoke to the guards, who stepped aside to let them pass.

Following Jaya through the doorway, Red Feather took a moment to gather his bearings. It seemed like only a few hours had passed since the ceremony of the serpent during the setting sun. But the gentle light of the coming sunrise spread across the horizon. Looking up, Red Feather saw the stars become faint.

Have I been awake all night? Has time truly passed so quickly?

When Red Feather climbed the pyramid last night, the sun had set and everything surrounding the city of Xazaa had been plunged into darkness. He remembered the brightness of the torches held by the thousands of people surrounding the pyramid and filling all the avenues leading to it. The city itself had been full of light, but he couldn't see the crops or jungle beyond it.

Now in the early light of day, Red Feather beheld the wonder of the view from the top of the pyramid.

Whoever made the model of the Land of

Swamp Dragons that rested on the table inside the pyramid must have stood here to create it. The jungle stretched deep and wide. In the far distance, temples like this one peeked above the tree line in all directions, each denoting a different city.

Noting where the sun prepared to rise, Red Feather turned his back to it and pointed at the nearest temple to the west. "Is that where I'm going?"

Jaya looked into his eyes and then kissed his cheek.

For a brief moment, panic seized Red Feather. How could he communicate to Jaya that he needed to find Greeta? How could he explain that his feelings were for Greeta, not Jaya?

And what would Jaya, the new king of Xazaa, do if she understood his intentions?

When Jaya gazed into his eyes again, Red Feather's worries melted. Although Red Feather came from a large family where he had many brothers, he'd seen in other families the fondness that passed from sister to brother. He saw that same type of fondness in Jaya's eyes right now.

He struggled to imagine what Jaya must be feeling. The anguish of seeing her father murdered in front of her. The pain of failing to reach him in time to help. The sudden and unexpected weight of a city and perhaps an entire nation on her shoulders. The uncertainty of what Fine-hurst and his smoke dragon might do next.

Red Feather believed that even though Jaya might not understand every word he said, she would see his heart when he spoke. "Don't worry, my sister," Red Feather said. "I will help you and your nation."

CHAPTER 26

The yellow-painted woman Kaypahl led her fellow priestesses and the Foretold One toward the Temple of the Seven Mystics. Her argument with the local guards and those from Xazaa left her shaken. When she recognized the tall blonde woman, Kaypahl knew she had to take action.

And yet mystical prophecies tended toward the delicate.

Just because the woman looked like the Foretold One didn't mean she *was* the Foretold One. Tests must be conducted to confirm or deny her identity.

Of course, there was no point trying to explain that to the guards.

Kaypahl snorted at the thought. The type of men who became guards liked taking action first and asking questions later, if at all. They might not laugh in front of the priestesses, but the guards didn't hesitate to laugh behind the women's backs.

Such clumsy and peculiar men. Kaypahl didn't understand why the guards had no problem believing in the rain and thunder gods but ridiculed the prophecies of those gods.

It made no sense.

Kaypahl paused when the Whispering Voice spoke inside her head.

Get ready. The girl will run.

At such times, Kaypahl behaved more like a guard than a priestess: she took action first and asked questions later. She saw the long hooked poles used for closing the wooden shutters of the temple window openings stored horizontally on hooks attached to the building. Kaypahl dashed toward the poles and grabbed one.

At the same time, the other priestesses shouted in surprise.

City center! the Whispering Voice told Kaypahl.

Following the voice's guidance, Kaypahl ran in the direction of the center of the city with the hooked pole in hand.

The blonde woman bolted in that same direction.

On her heels, Kaypahl swung the long pole against the blonde's legs, making her stumble and lose ground. Kaypahl caught up and hooked the woman's knees, forcing her to fall.

As always, Kaypahl gave silent thanks to the Whispering Voice for its good and true guidance.

The blonde tried to wriggle free, but the other priestesses arrived in time to make it clear she had nowhere to run. The woman shouted at them and pointed in the direction where her friends had been taken.

"We should take pity on her," one of the priestesses said. "Can't we at least let her know her friends will be safe?"

"How?" another woman said. "She can't understand anything we say."

Kaypahl said, "It doesn't matter that she can't communicate with us. We all know the directives. We can't assume she's the Foretold One until the tests prove it beyond doubt."

Another priestess said, "At the very least she should know we'll release her along with her friends if she is not the Foretold One."

"That's impossible," Kaypahl said. "Giving her information of any kind would interfere with the testing process."

A few of the priestesses sighed in regret, which made the blonde woman stare at them with a face drawn in confusion.

"Look at her," Kaypahl said. "We are not doing her any favors. We should be neutral in our dealings with the woman. Be neither warm nor cold. Be neither kind nor cruel."

The blonde woman watched Kaypahl and the other women. Dismissing the others, the blonde spoke directly to Kaypahl and gestured back toward the gate. "Xazaa," the blonde woman said. She then hesitated and looked around as if in search of something. Her face brightened and she picked up a handful of dirt. Standing tall, she let the dirt fall, which created a cloud. The blonde woman dropped to the ground and crawled with her elbows and knees bowed out like a dragon.

"Look!" one of the priestesses cried. "She's showing us what is foretold!"

Another priestess pointed at the blonde woman and said, "She's walking like a dragon. How can we ignore that?"

Smiling, the blonde woman stood and faced Kaypahl with crossed arms and an air of confidence while the priestesses babbled in excitement.

Kaypahl took a moment to study the woman's appearance. The height that allowed her to tower over the Swamp Lander women. The long blonde hair. The blue eyes that leaned toward lavender. The fierce determination on her face.

She looked like every image of the Foretold One that Kaypahl had ever seen.

And then there was the fact that she'd quickly identified Kaypahl as the leader of the priestesses by speaking directly to her and no one else.

But the Whispering Voice remained quiet. Wouldn't it tell Kaypahl if the Foretold One stood before her?

"Enough!" Kaypahl said, commanding silence. "We all know how foolish it can be to make assumptions. Perhaps she is the Foretold One. Perhaps she is not."

The priestesses took on an air of dejection and murmured their understanding and agreement.

Watching them, the blonde trembled. But within moments, her face took on an even grimmer expression of determination.

Kaypahl felt her own grim determination and hoped it showed on her face. "We should waste no time. Prepare her for the first test."

While the other priestesses led the blonde into the temple, Kaypahl headed for the pyramid behind it.

After passing through the pyramid's entrance, Kaypahl returned to the chamber to continue her meeting with the new king of Xazaa. Taking a seat, Kaypahl said, "She's here."

Jaya nodded. Unlike the winding route she'd instructed her guards to take, Jaya had traveled the most direct path from Xazaa, much of it underground. "Then summon the smoke dragon that killed my father so we can destroy it."

How odd. A day filled with delicate sit-

uations.

Kaypahl had no desire to insult the new king, even though the young woman failed to recognize her own haste. Better to offer subtle guidance to a new king than antagonize one. "I trust everything you told me, Jaya. I regret you witnessed your father's death."

Tears welled in the new king's eyes. "We'll all feel better once we have vengeance."

And there is the difference between Xazaa and us. They seek revenge, but we seek spiritual order. They are driven by the rawness of their feelings of pain at the death of their king. Our responsibility is to follow the directives so that we may fulfill the promise our gods made to other gods.

But how do I guide Jaya while still showing my respect for her kingship?

"I remember when war ruled our land," Kaypahl said. "But now we live in peace."

Jaya's grim expression remained fixed.

"When I was a girl, Xazaa had no king," Kaypahl continued. "But we needed one when Xazaa entered into the peace agreement with other cities. And we chose your family because it is one of cool heads and wise hearts."

Jaya rubbed a hand over her face, and the grimness disappeared.

"I believe you're right in recognizing this blonde woman as the one our gods tell us we are obligated to help," Kaypahl said.

"Of course it's her," Jaya said. "It must be her."

Kaypahl nodded to signal her agreement. "And yet our gods tell us we must test her to be sure."

Anger flared in Jaya's eyes. "You doubt my judgment?"

"Not at all." Kaypahl cleared her throat to give her time to mull over the best way to win Jaya over. "But neither do I doubt the judgment of the gods, who say we must take steps to be certain that we identify the Foretold One correctly. For all we know, this woman could be in league with the smoke dragon. She might be one of his agents who disguised herself as the Foretold One. If we assume she's the Foretold One without testing her for the sake of validating who she is, all our lives will be at risk."

Jaya chewed the end of her thumb. "I see."

With an assuring voice, Kaypahl said, "We will summon the smoke dragon. But we must first do everything within our power to protect ourselves."

When Jaya nodded her agreement, Kaypahl should have felt relaxed.

Instead, she considered the extreme

danger of waiting to summon the smoke dragon. Based on the information Jaya brought, the creature must be somewhere in the surrounding jungles right now.

Jaya is right, and she knows it. We should summon the smoke dragon immediately and destroy it. The longer we wait, the more likely it is to find and annihilate us.

But as much as she longed to do what the new king wanted, Kaypahl's responsebilities were to the gods, not to kings.

Or to what Kaypahl believed would be best.

For the first time in many years, Kaypahl wished she had nothing to do with the gods and the demands they placed upon mortals such as her.

CHAPTER 27

Greeta's frustration grew by the moment. She didn't understand why she'd been separated from Frayka and Njall or why Yellow Skin tripped her when Greeta made a break to run where she thought her friends were being held.

The other women escorted Greeta into a tiny stone room with a high ceiling inside the temple. A heavy wooden door closed and locked in place behind her. Greeta shouted and pounded on the door, but it wouldn't budge.

Stay calm. Is there any way to get out?

Greeta found she could walk from one end of the room to the other in three paces. It had no window openings, but small bowls of fire rested on a ledge high above her reach. The ledge ran alongside each wall, and a fire bowl lit up every wall. She examined the floor and every wall but found no means of escape.

I'm trapped.

Greeta felt her heart race while wondering when she would see daylight again. She gulped air too quickly because the room seemed like a tomb.

I have to get out.

One after the other, the contents of the fire bowls cracked and popped.

Looking up in surprise, Greeta saw bright yellow smoke spill out of the bowls and descend toward the floor. The smoke collected in puddles around her feet. The scent of wildflowers caught her off guard.

Suddenly feeling woozy, Greeta steadied her hand against the wall for support. Even so, the room seemed to spin around her.

Moments later, she fainted. When Greeta collapsed, her body disappeared into the yellow smoke billowing across the floor.

* * *

Now unconscious, it would take some time before Greeta understood she had entered the Dreamtime.

Greeta walked outside the pyramid behind the temple, finding the entire city deserted.

"Frayka!" she shouted. "Njall! Where are you?"

Greeta's voice echoed throughout the

plaza and empty avenues surrounding the pyramid. From the clear sky above, the sun warmed her skin. Her nose twitched at the scent of wildflowers.

The smoke!

With a start, Greeta realized the last thing she remembered was being locked inside a tiny room inside the temple and being enveloped by bright yellow smoke.

Did they poison me? Am I dead?

A muffled cry floated through the air.

Greeta looked everywhere but saw no one. Only the pyramid blocked her view of the rest of the city. Maybe someone stood on the other side of the pyramid.

With every step Greeta took, a small puff of yellow smoke floated up from where her foot touched the plaza's stone pavement. When she reached the opposite side of the pyramid, she gaped in surprise.

The Shining Star shaman Shadow stood on a platform halfway up the side of the pyramid.

"Shadow!" Greeta shouted and waved. "It's me!"

When Shadow nodded her recognition, Greeta saw that someone had bound and gagged the shaman.

"Don't worry!" Greeta cried. "I'll help you."

But when Greeta turned to run up the pyramid's steps, she realized it had none. Instead, its sides slanted smoothly up to

Shadow's platform, which stood at four times Greeta's height.

Befuddled, Greeta thought about the pyramid in Xazaa, certain that each of its four sides had a center stairway leading up to the top.

There must be steps on the other sides. Once I climb those steps I can figure out how to get to Shadow.

Greeta retraced her steps, staring at each side of the pyramid when she encountered it. Each side had a completely smooth surface and no steps. Greeta circled the structure, baffled by what she saw.

I don't understand. If there are no steps at all, how did Shadow get up there?

A new thought struck Greeta. She shouted at Shadow, "Are we in the Dreamtime?"

Shadow nodded, confirming Greeta's suspicion.

Finally, everything Greeta saw made sense. After all, Shadow was the one who taught Greeta how to walk in the Dreamtime. She said Greeta had a gift to give to the world. Greeta assumed that gift had something to do with the Dreamtime, but Shadow had vanished and Greeta never had the chance to learn more.

So far, Greeta's experiences in the Dreamtime had been mostly with ghosts. Margreet used the Dreamtime to teach

Greeta how to use a sword. And her mother Astrid provided details about Greeta's past as well as advice.

But why would Shadow appear in the Dreamtime like this? It didn't make any sense.

"Do you need help?" Greeta said. "Are you in danger?"

Shadow shook her head from side to side: no.

Greeta paced in front of the pyramid, trying to understand why she had entered the Dreamtime and why Shadow appeared in a place where Greeta couldn't reach her. "Can you talk to me?" Greeta shouted. "Can you join me down here?"

Again, Shadow shook her head: no.

Greeta focused, struggling to puzzle out the situation. She wanted to ask more pointed questions. But until Shadow had the ability to speak, Greeta's questions would have to be phrased for yes or no answers.

"Are you here to guide me?"

No.

"Are you here to help me?"

Shadow hesitated and failed to answer.

"Do you want to help me?"

Shadow nodded yes.

Greeta stared at Shadow and the pyramid as if the answer might be right in front of her. Once again, Greeta lamented her inability to control shifting her shape into a dragon. If she were a dragon, she could climb up the side of the pyramid with ease.

That thought startled Greeta.

Do I have to become a dragon to climb? Or can I do it in my mortal shape?

She placed her hands on the side of the pyramid. Although the sloping wall had a smooth appearance, the stones had a texture rough enough to grip.

Reaching high, Greeta ran her fingertips along the seam where two stones met and discovered an open space into which she could slide her fingers. Gripping the top edge of one stone, Greeta stepped onto the wall and discovered she could hold herself in place. One foot after another, she walked up to another seam where she wedged her toes and then reached up to find a new handhold.

Taking a slow and methodical approach, Greeta hauled herself up the side of the pyramid. The stones above her no longer looked smooth, because carvings of kings and monsters appeared on them.

Greeta reminded herself she was in the Dreamtime, where anything could change at any time.

The carvings offered her better grips, making it easier to climb. When Greeta reached the platform, she hoisted herself up onto it. Carvings covered the platform on which she now stood. Greeta freed the shaman from the gag around her mouth and the ties binding her arms.

But Shadow didn't act like her usual jubilant self. Instead, her manner struck Greeta as dark and foreboding.

"Everything is not as it seems," Shadow said.

The base of the pyramid trembled beneath the platform on which they stood. Worry crossed the shaman's face.

Feeling the platform shift beneath her feet, Greeta looked down to see the carvings come to life and stand up from the stones.

The stone carving of a fearsome king climbed to his feet between Greeta and Shadow. His body had a depth no greater than Greeta's forefinger, making him look flat but solid. His eyes were dark pits carved into his stone face, surrounded by an elaborate headdress. He raised a weapon that looked like an ax.

Greeta dodged around the strange figure to join Shadow's side. "We'll climb down. Follow me."

The carving of a monster with massive wings curled up from the platform floor. It lifted its wings high and opened its beak, but no sound came out. The monster lunged forward and snapped its beak.

Tugging Shadow's hand, Greeta headed for the platform edge. "Follow me! Now!"

"I can't." Shadow's hand slipped away

from Greeta's grip.

When Greeta turned and tried to hold onto Shadow's hand, she saw the shaman evaporate into white mist drifting toward the sky. Before Greeta could do anything else, the fearsome king clamped his stone hand around her wrist, and the monster surrounded them with its wings.

CHAPTER 28

While the morning sun climbed high overhead, Red Feather trekked through the jungle on a narrow trail with his plant slung across his back in swaddling clothes that tied across his chest. Although trees shaded his path, the thick humidity made sweat bead on his forehead. Behind him, the steady sound of claws dragging against the ground gave Red Feather both comfort and trepidation.

When he left Xazaa hours ago, Jaya ordered her dragons to accompany him. Red Feather hoped they might offer protection instead of devouring him.

Red Feather paused to study the sun before it centered itself in the sky. He recalled the model of the Land of Swamp Dragons that Jaya showed to him. He visualized the path he needed to take from

Xazaa to the small temple city where he should find Greeta.

Does this have something to do with her ability to turn into a dragon? Do the Swamp Landers know she can do that? Is that why they have a painting of her inside Jaya's pyramid?

Red Feather shook those questions out of his head. Answers would come in due time. For now, he had to focus on finding Greeta.

Squinting at the sun and then back at the direction from which he'd come, Red Feather suspected the trail should bear to the left soon. Otherwise, he might have to forge his own path.

Ready to move forward, Red Feather stopped at the sudden silence. He heard no birds chirping or insects buzzing. The dragons following him no longer made a sound.

Red Feather felt the hair on the back of his neck stand up. He gripped the hilt of the stone knife tucked under his belt.

A low growl rumbled a short distance ahead.

A large black animal with the heft of a man stepped onto the path. Snarling, it revealed a mouthful of sharp teeth. It pawed at the ground with deadly claws. Its bright green eyes showed no mercy.

Red Feather shuddered and caught himself from taking a few steps back. He knew even the smallest retreat would cause any animal to attack.

The black animal threatening him resembled a mountain lion, an animal known in the Shining Star nation.

"Chaca!" Red Feather called the names of the dragons behind him. "Zolten!"

The jungle remained silent, and Red Feather faced the black animal alone.

The leaves on the plant strapped to his back tapped his shoulder.

"Not now," Red Feather said. "We're in danger." He stood perfectly still, knowing his best hope of fighting the animal would be to slash his knife toward its vulnerable belly. That meant the animal would have to expose its underside to him. And that would most likely happen when the animal took a leap toward him.

The plant's tapping became more insistent.

The black animal's gaze shifted from Red Feather's eyes to the leaves grazing his shoulder. The animal sniffed the air.

Is the plant trying to tell me something?

Instead of reaching for his knife, Red Feather shifted his hand up to his shoulder until he felt the familiar touch of the plant.

The black animal licked its lips, and its green eyes brightened with anticipation.

Several leaves wrapped tightly around Red Feather's fingers and hands. The tension between his hand and the plant eased when he felt the stems of the leaves break loose.

Thinking back to the images he'd seen on the walls inside Jaya's pyramid, Red Feather remembered the picture showing how the plant attacked the smoke dragon with its leaves. They seemed to fly like arrows. The leaves had pierced the smoke dragon and caused it to burst into dust.

And that dust had fallen to the ground and created a trail for the warrior who had emerged from the mouth of the serpent of the pyramid.

A new possibility struck Red Feather.

Has the smoke dragon taken a new form? Is this animal in front of me really the smoke dragon in disguise?

Red Feather jerked his leaf-covered hand at the black animal. "Attack!" he said to the leaves.

Instead of flying like arrows, they drifted high in the air as if picked up by a strong wind. They floated toward the black animal.

Still bright with interest, the animal's green eyes followed the path of the floating leaves.

Relieved that the animal no longer seemed to realize he existed, Red Feather took a step back.

The black animal's head snapped toward him. It growled again, and padded toward him.

The leaves dipped down around the animal's head. One leaf touched its nose.

Shifting its attention back to the floating leaves, the black animal stood on its hind legs and batted its front paws at the leaves.

One leaf swooped down and tickled the animal's belly.

The gigantic cat jumped straight up in the air. It grinned in surprise and delight. When the animal landed on the ground, it squirmed on its back, offering its belly to the leaves.

The leaves shot down at the black animal. But instead of impaling the large cat, the vegetation tickled it. In response, the animal kept squirming and batted playfully at its attackers until they tired it. When the black cat rolled onto its belly and rested its chin on its front paws, the leaves landed on its nose. After sniffing them, the animal ate the leaves and drifted to sleep.

"Thank you, my dear friend," Red Feather whispered to the plant he carried on his back.

The two dragons bounded from the trail behind Red Feather and joined his side. They grunted fiercely at the sleeping cat.

Red Feather leaned down to whisper to the dragons. "Quiet. All we have to do is walk past it. The beast might sleep for a good while. And when it detects your scent, I think it will leave us be."

One of the dragons looked at Red Feather while the other scratched at the ground with its claws.

"Fine," Red Feather said. "I'll lead the way. But stay close on my heels this time."

Taking tentative steps, Red Feather eased his way past the sleeping cat. He gestured for the dragons to follow.

Mimicking Red Feather, they took tentative steps forward and flanked the sleeping animal. But instead of walking past it, the dragons attacked it.

Startled awake, the gigantic cat fought back, baring its fangs and exposing its long, sharp claws. But neither caused any damage beyond superficial scratches to the dragons' scales. Just as Red Feather planned to do should he need to defend himself, the dragons flipped the black animal on its back and ripped into its belly.

Slumping with disappointment, Red Feather said, "You don't have to kill it!"

Then again, the dragons are animals. This is the way of nature for animals.

A worried thought crossed his mind.

But the dragons don't obey me the way they obey Jaya. Does being away from her make them disobedient? Or are they reluctant to listen to me the way they listen to her?

Red Feather found a fallen log and sat on it. To his green and leafy companion, he said, "I suppose they've worked up a hunger. We might as well let them eat."

CHAPTER 29

Greeta wanted to scream when the stone monster wrapped its unforgiving wings around her, but she dropped to the pyramid's platform instead.

I'm in the Dreamtime. This isn't real.

The world went dark, and silence surrounded her.

* * *

A patch of yellow paint on her arm looked smudged, and Kaypahl used her fingertips to smooth it out. She studied the shaman named Shadow who knelt by the figure of the Foretold One lying in the smallest room of the temple.

Since the shaman arrived, she learned some of the Swamp Lander language, and Kaypahl knew some of the Shining Star language. She drummed up the best words she could think of. "Woman here now?"

Shadow knelt by the side of the tall and pale woman. The shaman held one of the Foretold One's hands and stroked it. Shadow looked up at Kaypahl and smiled when she replied in her own Shining Star language. "Out of Dreamtime."

Kaypahl nodded her approval. Everyone in the Great Turtle Lands understood the Dreamtime. Kaypahl's entrance into the duty of becoming a priestess required a walk in the Dreamtime. With the aid of a Swamp Land shaman, she had done so. Mostly, Kaypahl found the Dreamtime akin to going for a walk and ending up with her feet stuck in mud. Such an uneventful experience made Kaypahl fear she failed to qualify as a priestess.

Instead, the Temple of the Seven Mystics accepted her immediately. Kaypahl joined the priestesses who acted as intermediaries between the king of Xazaa and the gods.

Not knowing enough words of the Shining Star language, Kaypahl asked, "How long?" She then pointed at the Foretold One and pantomimed waking up from sleep.

"Soon," Shadow said.

Kaypahl switched to her own language, knowing the shaman would understand. "Come with me." She led the way into the adjacent room and joined the other priestesses already gathered there.

All the walls surrounding them were painted black. Kaypahl picked out a small specimen from a bowl filled with chalky rocks. When Shadow approached her, Kaypahl handed the rock to her and gestured to the walls. "Show us what you saw."

Nodding her understanding, Shadow walked to a wall and used the chalk rock to draw pictures showing what she experienced with Greeta in the Dreamtime. When Shadow drew the image of Greeta figuring out how to climb up the sloping side of the pyramid, the priestesses chattered with excitement.

"Look at how she passed the test!" said a priestess painted in blue. "Look at her cleverness!"

"And her intent to help the shaman," another priestess said. "Only the Foretold One would do these things. Most others would give up easily and believe the shaman couldn't be helped. Or run away to save themselves and leave the shaman behind."

"Most others would do that," Kaypahl said. She took the legend of the Foretold One very seriously. She also took her responsibility to protect not only the people of the Seven Mystics City seriously but her duty to protect these priestesses and herself. "That is why we have three tests to conduct. This test doesn't tell us enough about her."

While the priestesses continued with their happy chatter, Kaypahl studied the rest of the images that the shaman continued to draw on the wall. The final images gave her pause. Kaypahl sidled up to the shaman and asked questions.

The shaman confirmed Kaypahl's suspicions. She worried about the image of the carvings lifting from the face of the pyramid in Shadow's drawings. Kaypahl suspected such an event indicated a threat, even if that event took place in the Dreamtime. She wondered if that threat would be directed at the Foretold One or the City of the Seven Mystics.

Or both.

* * *

Although Greeta's head felt thick with grogginess, she became aware of the priestesses helping her from the floor. They guided Greeta into another room inside the temple and sat her on a small bench at a table running the length of the room. She gripped the edge of the table to keep from falling over.

The priestesses left the room and locked the door in place behind them.

The table presented a meal made of cooked small grains, corn, and a strange type of bread steamed on a flat stone plate with curved edges. Breathing deeply, Greeta recognized the scent of some spices she'd encountered in the Land of Swamp Dragons. One had an earthy sweetness. Another made her nose twitch with a tickling sensation.

Greeta's stomach grumbled. It made her realize she hadn't eaten since yesterday afternoon. Her hunger convinced her to take the risk of eating. She ripped apart the slightly stiff bread and appreciated the sharp and sour tang of its spices. The corn and grains benefitted from herbs that made her tongue numb. After she'd devoured the food, the curved edges of the stone plate contained a small amount of broth. Greeta picked up the plate and drank the broth from its curved edge.

Once finished, Greeta held the stone plate still when she saw what someone had hidden beneath it on the table: a lock of blonde hair held together with a narrow leather tie. The color was a few shades darker than Greeta's hair. She recognized it at once.

Njall's hair.

Why would anyone cut Njall's hair?

Or is this a message that he and Frayka need my help and someone here is willing to make that happen?

Greeta picked up the lock of hair with one hand and replaced the stone plate on the table with the other. A stream of daylight fell across the tabletop. She saw only solid stone walls in front and to either side.

Turning around, Greeta looked back to see narrow window openings carved high into the wall behind her.

There might be enough space for me to squeeze through.

First, Greeta tied the lock of hair around her own. If someone in this city left Njall's hair as a message, then Greeta wanted no one else to find that message. Keeping it to herself would protect the Northlanders as well as the one who appeared to help them.

A heated but muffled conversation began on the other side of the locked door.

Reaching toward the window opening, her fingertips grazed its bottom edge. Greeta jumped, but she couldn't find enough purchase to bear her weight.

She remembered the small bench she'd used to sit at the table. Although carved from stone, its surface felt light and airy to the touch, just like the stone so porous that it soaked up the rainfall.

Greeta struggled to drag the small bench across the floor. She placed it under the opening and stood on the bench, now able to place her hands on the bottom ledge. But when she tried to lift herself, her strength failed.

Everyone knew very specific differences between women and men existed. One such difference was about strength. A man's strength came from his arms and chest. A woman's strength came from her legs.

Greeta jumped and tried to pull herself into the opening but failed again.

The conversation outside the room grew louder. The door rattled as if someone brushed against it.

Greeta assessed what she had: a table, a bench, and a stone plate.

The table is too large to move, and it looks much heavier than the bench. I've already placed the bench in the best way to use it. And I don't see how a stone plate can help me.

The feel of the bench beneath her feet reminded Greeta of a pond surrounded by such rocks near her Shining Star home. She remembered how Auntie Peppa taught her to swim. And how Papa taught Greeta to stand on such a rock, bend her knees, and push against it to dive into the water.

The locked door rattled louder.

Greeta bent her knees and pushed off the bench to jump higher and stronger. As if diving into water, she reached through the opening and grasped the far side of its ledge.

This time, she succeeded.

Greeta scrambled through the narrow opening and looked outside. Luckily no one guarded this side of the temple. She saw people walking through the city behind the temple, but no one noticed her.

Easing her way through the opening, Greeta sat on its outer edge and glanced at the ground below.

She stilled at the sight of a garden of jagged rocks beneath her.

If I'd jumped without looking, I could have broken my legs! Jumping onto those rocks might have even killed me!

Greeta reconsidered her predicament.

Those priestesses are toying with me. What if they're trying to find ways to kill me for their amusement?

I have to get out of this city.

Greeta inched her way to the edge. When she jumped, she pushed off the side of the building to propel her body forward. When Greeta landed safely on the ground, she looked back and realized she'd barely cleared the garden of jagged rocks.

Now all she had to do was find Frayka and Njall.

CHAPTER 30

Greeta's heart pounded so loud she thought she could hear it.

She studied her surroundings while crouching outside the back wall of the temple. A short time ago, Greeta and her Northlander friends had entered the gates of the city, which were now out of sight because those gates stood on the opposite side of the temple.

The pyramid loomed before her, although it looked much smaller than the pyramid in Xazaa. Like that larger city, this one had little greenery. Paved avenues and plazas surrounded the pyramid at the city's center.

Although no sound came from the opening through which she had crawled, Greeta believed she had little time to figure out how to find Frayka and Njall. The priestesses were bound to realize she'd escaped. Greeta had to make a decision and move quickly.

She observed the people moving throughout the city. It didn't have a large marketplace like Xazaa. The few residents walking through the plazas and avenues appeared to be men on their way to work in the fields outside the city walls.

Although tempted to walk in the open as if she belonged, Greeta knew her height and appearance would draw too much attention. Instead, she decided to take the chance of walking along the base of the pyramid towering before her. That way, the structure would hide her not only from the temple but from most of the people in the city.

Greeta crossed the wide avenue separating the temple from the pyramid. She then turned the corner of the pyramid that best blocked the temple's view of her. She walked so close to the base of the pyramid that she could reach out and touch its sloping side.

Put one foot in front of the other. Keep moving. Pay attention to everything happening, but don't act suspicious.

Greeta strained to remember their arrival at the gate this morning and how she'd been separated from Frayka and Njall. Everything happened so quickly. But she remembered her friends being taken across the expanse of the city in the direction of a small stone house.

The pyramid must be blocking my view of that house. Once I reach the next corner, I'll probably see it.

But then what?

Greeta considered her options. If her friends were guarded, Greeta could confront the guard. But that would probably end with Greeta being escorted back to the temple from which she had just escaped.

When she walked the length of the pyramid's side, Greeta approached the upcoming corner with caution. A small group of men strolled through the plaza ahead. She timed looking around the corner of the pyramid with the pace of the men. Sure enough, when Greeta peeked around the corner she saw the men pass in front of the stone house where Frayka and Njall had been taken.

Taking a step back, Greeta crouched by the pyramid.

Two men stood guard in front of the stone house. Each held a shoulder-high wooden spear with a flat stone spearhead. She considered her situation.

I'm alone. I have no weapon. If I step away from the pyramid, they'll see me. If I retreat, the women from the temple are likely to find me.

The first solution Greeta considered was turning into a dragon. If she could transform into a dangerous animal, she could charge the building that held her friends prisoner, knock the guards aside, and break the door down with one flip of her tail.

Because Greeta didn't know what had caused her to turn into a dragon, she focused on remembering all the things that led up to that event. She recalled her range of emotions about Finehurst: from wondering if he might be the love of her life to questioning his character to losing her temper with him. Could that have been what triggered her shifting shape? Her anger?

Greeta drummed up everything she could think of that would contribute to a good rage. She thought about the ceremony of the serpent in Xazaa and how Finehurst's smoke dragon destroyed everything, including the king. She remembered pushing her way through the crowd in an attempt to stop the smoke dragon only to be exiled from the city without Red Feather. The Xazaa guards forced her through the jungle with Frayka and Njall but then made them lead the way after an unexpected encounter with an animal endangered them all. And once they'd arrived in this smaller city, she'd been separated from her friends and didn't know if they were safe.

Trembling with rage, Greeta looked at

her body.

She still looked mortal. Nothing indicated she might turn into a dragon.

Maybe Finehurst didn't have anything to do with it. Greeta considered that Red Feather had been present each time she shapeshifted. And hadn't it been Red Feather who told her that the Shining Star people recognized the existence of shapeshifters and honored them? Greeta shuddered at the memory.

Still, she looked mortal.

She wracked her brain, trying to come up with some other reason that might have been the catalyst for her becoming a dragon. No matter how hard she thought, nothing made any sense.

Maybe I don't have to take the shape of a dragon to fight like one.

The strange thought startled her. If she couldn't gain an advantage by changing into a large and dangerous animal, how could she possibly fight like one?

Greeta felt helpless without her sword. She'd left it in Red Feather's healing building when they went to the serpent ceremony in Xazaa. It didn't make sense to attempt fighting the guards unarmed.

A different memory occurred to Greeta. One involving things Margreet taught her in the Dreamtime: techniques for using one's own sword and techniques for wrestling away the sword from one's opponent.

Before she could lose her nerve, Greeta stepped around the corner of the pyramid and walked directly toward the two guards with a smile on her face.

One guard pointed at her and nudged his companion. The guards aimed their spears at her.

Greeta slowed her pace but kept her smile. "Hello, Men. You don't understand me, and I hope you're feeling confused. The more confused you are, the easier this will be." Once Greeta stood close enough for the guards to hurt her with a forward thrust of a spear, she stopped.

One guard spoke to her angrily.

Greeta took a step back and gestured for him to follow.

The guard exchanged words with his colleague. They split up and circled Greeta from different directions: one moved to her right while the other eased to her left.

Greeta lunged toward the closer guard, stepped past the spearhead, and clamped her hands around the spear. She yanked the wooden pole forward, causing the guard to topple onto his knees. Still clutching the spear, Greeta placed one foot on his back and kicked the guard onto his chest. His head hit the pavement hard enough to knock him unconscious.

When the other guard cried out and ran toward her, Greeta surprised him by dropping to the ground. By the time he stopped his momentum, Greeta found him close enough to deliver a well-placed kick to his knees. Crying out in pain, the guard's legs crumpled, and he fell on his face.

Moving quickly, Greeta gathered both spears and ran toward the building. Narrow window openings lined the top of each wall. If inside, her friends would be able to hear Greeta's voice. "Frayka!" Greeta shouted. "Njall! Where are you?"

Greeta held her breath so that the sound of it wouldn't interfere with her ability to hear them answer. When she heard nothing in response, she ran around the building to another side and another set of openings. "Frayka! Njall!" Again, she heard no sound inside the building.

She heard a distant groan and worried that one of the guards must be regaining consciousness.

Greeta had to move quickly. She called her friends' names while she ran around the corner of the building but stopped cold when she saw it had no window openings. Remembering the building's entrance, she realized it had no openings either. Baffled, she said, "What have they done with you?"

A faint voice shouted, "Greeta!"

Chilled by the sound, Greeta knew it didn't come from inside the building. But she saw no other place anywhere nearby. A plaza and many avenues surrounded it. The pyramid stood as its nearest neighbor, and the voice came from a different direction.

"Frayka?" Greeta said, hoping her friend hadn't been killed and now spoke to her as a ghost. "Where are you?"

"Look down!" Frayka cried. "We're below ground!"

Hope burst through Greeta like the sun brightening a cloudy day. She walked toward the sound of Frayka's voice, all the while studying the stone pavement beneath her feet.

There!

She spotted one pavestone that looked different. Spaces that might be handholds had been carved on either side. Greeta knelt by the unusual pavestone. "Frayka?"

"Yes! We're here!"

Greeta bent over and slipped her hands through the open spaces in the pavestone, but when she tried to lift it she found its weight too great and felt the strain in her back. Greeta sat and placed her feet on either side of the pavestone so that one handhold rested between her feet while the other was closer to her body.

Grasping the handhold between her feet, Greeta felt the strain once more in her back but succeeded in lifting one edge slightly. When her back protested in pain, she released the stone. "Frayka! Can you push up on this stone?"

"We stand too deep," Njall answered.

"It's too far above our reach."

Greeta threaded both hands into the other handhold, close to her body. With her feet still planted on either side of the pavestone, she felt the strain in her arms this time.

A new thought struck her.

Greeta kneeled so that she straddled the handhold while sitting on her heels. With one smooth motion, she stood on her knees, using the force of her entire body to lift the pavestone. She felt the weight of the stone come up with her hands and then flip over to reveal an open space into the darkness below.

But before Greeta could call out again to her friends, she felt a blow to the back of her head.

Hands pushed her forward into the dark, open space.

CHAPTER 31

Red Feather continued through the jungle until he saw a tall stone gate guarded by two men a good distance ahead. Confident the guards hadn't seen him, Red Feather stepped off the path and into the surrounding vegetation. Behind him, a tree covered in curling white bark twisted like an old man. Large purple flowers grew among its roots. A tiny bird hovered among them and dipped its long beak into their nectar. When Red Feather stepped on a fallen twig, the bird looked up and then zipped away.

Broad and leafy plants rustled around his feet and turned toward the similar plant he carried on his back.

The two dragons trotted along the path and paused when they realized Red Feather had stepped away from it. They nosed the vegetation in which he stood but kept their distance. One of the dragons lifted its nose high in the air and paused. Moments later, it galloped toward Red Feather with the other dragon close on its heels.

Red Feather ducked low to the ground. He hoped the commotion created by the dragons plummeting through the jungle wouldn't attract the attention of the guards. The animals ran just beyond Red Feather and then halted. Both dragons nosed the ground and pawed at it. One of them looked up to give Red Feather a hopeful look.

What have the beasts discovered?

Kneeling next to the sniffing dragons, Red Feather ran a hand across a stone grate nestled into the ground and hidden by a thicket of bushes. The acrid scent of smoke drifted from the space below the grate.

Of course. That's what caught the dragons' attention. They smelled smoke.

Peering closer through the slats in the stone grate, Red Feather realized a soft glow of light illuminated the underground space below.

One of the dragons scraped its claws across the grate. The other dragon nosed the stone edges that rested neatly into the dirt surrounding it.

Red Feather had recognized intelligence in the dragons' eyes long ago. Sometimes their thoughts appeared obvious. Right now, he would swear they were trying to convince him to lift the grate and explore the grounds below.

Peering through the jungle foliage at the distant gate and its guards, Red Feather wondered how they might receive him. Jaya convinced him that Greeta took this path, which meant he'd find her on the other side of the gate.

But if Greeta arrived here, why hadn't Red Feather met the Xazaa guards who escorted her? Shouldn't they have returned to Xazaa and wouldn't he meet them on this path? What reason would they have to stay? Were the guards being held against their will?

Unease overwhelmed Red Feather.

If Greeta and her friends need my help, then I can't hesitate. The time to decide is now.

Red Feather threaded his hands through the slots in the grate. He angled it up until one of the dragons knocked it away. The stone grate fell on the soft ground. One at a time, the dragons slithered through the opening.

Hoping to draw no attention to his presence, Red Feather dragged the stone grate back into place so that it once again covered the entrance to whatever might lie below ground. Again, he angled the grate up. He slipped through the opening and let the grate fall back into place above him.

Landing on his feet, Red Feather took a few moments to allow his vision to adjust from the harsh light of day to the soft and diffused light underground. The few thin streams of sunlight permitted by the grate revealed the rough, dark cave walls surrounding him.

When he raised his hands, Red Feather's fingertips grazed a low ceiling. Several steps forward brought him to a wall. Narrow passageways stretched to either side. He debated which direction might lead into the city.

The dragons trotted into the passageway to his right. Red Feather remembered his decision to trust them and followed the dragons.

They soon came across the light source. A stone pot pushed against one wall held a small fire. Another stone grate secured the ceiling above that fire, allowing the smoke to escape.

This must be the smoke the dragons smelled through the first grate we found.

But who placed the fire here? Who uses this secret passageway and for what purpose?

Red Feather examined the pot, the fire, and the surrounding area for clues but found none.

The dragons crowded him and sniffed

the fire. With satisfaction shining in their eyes, the dragons backed away from the fire and continued down the passageway.

Bringing up the rear, Red Feather saw light spreading far ahead.

This fire can't provide light that can travel that far. There must be another pot of fire. Perhaps the entire tunnel is filled with firepots.

When a second pot of fire appeared, the dragons repeated their inspection until once again satisfied. Red Feather gave the firepot no more than a glance because it appeared to be identical to the first one. He wondered why it held interest for the dragons until they came across another one.

The passageway widened and revealed a third pot of fire against the wall. Like the others, it stood beneath a stone grate in the ceiling.

The dragons hissed and circled the fire. Their tails whipped back and forth with such a vengeance that Red Feather took a step back to stay clear of them.

"What's wrong?" Red Feather asked the dragons. "What upsets you?"

Peering at the fire from a short distance, Red Feather saw nothing wrong with it. The stone pot and the flames it contained looked like the others. He looked up to see a stone grate above the fire, but he couldn't tell whether the city or the jungle was behind that grate.

But then Red Feather became aware of something peculiar. Clouds of brown smoke had drifted from the other fires. He remembered the way they climbed toward the grates and drifted through them.

No smoke escaped through this grate.

Instead, threads of black smoke snaked against the wall and ceiling. They slithered and intertwined.

The dragons eyed the smoke threads and snapped at them.

With a start, Red Feather remembered the images Jaya had shown him inside the Xazaa pyramid.

One image showed a warrior crawling out of the serpent's mouth. That warrior carried the same plant that Red Feather now carried on his back.

Jaya believes I'm the warrior in the picture.

Just like the king in the images, Jaya had placed her blood on the leaves before Red Feather left Xazaa. He'd watched the plant absorb her blood.

Jaya had shown him images of the warrior traveling through the jungle with the plant and fighting off terrifying animals.

That happened last night. The black mountain lion attacked, but the plant's leaves quelled the animal's anger. So far, everything Jaya showed me is coming true.

But one of Jaya's images showed the

warrior arriving at a gate and entering a small city at the foot of a grand temple with a base of stones carved with the image of a dragon.

I didn't enter the city through the gate. I'm underground instead.

Red Feather vividly remembered a picture showing a smoke dragon blocking the steps of the pyramid.

The black threads of smoke from the firepot wound together and leapt over the dragons. Taking the shape of a black smoke dragon, it blocked their path.

"Finehurst!" Red Feather shouted at the smoke dragon.

Jaya's dragons, Chaca and Zolten, bolted to confront the smoke dragon. They continued to thrash their tails and snap their jaws.

Red Feather's mind raced, struggling to put together everything he knew about Finehurst. He'd first met the man in the Shining Star nation, but Greeta told Red Feather she'd chased a shadow image of Finehurst: an illusion, not flesh and blood.

Red Feather saw that illusion yesterday. Although Red Feather first struggled to believe what Greeta told him about Finehurst, that doubt ended when he saw the smoke dragon murder the king of Xazaa.

And that same smoke dragon now blocked Red Feather's path, which meant the path must lead to the city and to Greeta.

"What do you want, Finehurst?" Red Feather said. Although he spoke to an illusion, he suspected it might be a messenger belonging to Finehurst.

The smoke dragon turned its head to glare at Red Feather. It then opened its jaws and spouted flames at Red Feather and Jaya's dragons, filling the space with fire and unbearable heat.

CHAPTER 32

Pushed through the opening she'd discovered in the city plaza, Greeta landed several feet below in darkness. Arms reached out to break the fall. But the blow to the back of her head knocked Greeta unconscious.

* * *

Greeta awoke in the Dreamtime. She recognized the Northlander village and the sound of iron hammering against an anvil. She turned to see her mother Astrid working in her smithery.

"Am I dead?" Greeta asked.

Astrid looked up and smiled at Greeta's approach. "No. Your visit here will be brief, but we have important things to talk about."

"Everything is falling apart," Greeta said. She sat on a bench near the anvil. "I don't know what to do."

"You don't know who you are," Astrid said. "You are torn between two cultures as different as fire and water." She brushed flakes of slag from the anvil surface with her gloved hand. "Northlanders are warriors, and Shining Star people are peaceful. You're afraid that if you choose the Northlands or the Shining Star nation that the people of the other culture will resent you. You're afraid you will lose the people you love in whatever culture you don't choose."

The truth of her mother's words ran down Greeta's throat like icy water, making her numb inside.

Astrid knelt and picked up a large white stone from the ground. "That's why you can't decide. But not deciding can kill you."

While Astrid centered the white stone on top of her anvil, black smoke from the forge fire climbed behind her.

Greeta stared at the smoke, frightened by the sight of it.

"You can't stand up inside your own skin until you decide who you are," Astrid said.

The black smoke hovering behind Astrid took the shape of a dragon.

Finehurst!

Greeta tried to speak, but fear constricted her voice into silence. She pointed frantically at the smoke.

Focused on her work, Astrid didn't see her. Astrid struck the stone with her hammer, pulverizing the stone into white dust.

The white dust drifted behind her and attached itself to the smoke dragon. The creature became so still that it looked like a statue suspended in mid-air.

Astrid brushed away a bit of white dust that lingered on the anvil. "But you don't have to choose to be the same every moment of every day. One moment it might be wise to be a Northlander. The next moment it might be wise to be Shining Star."

Greeta's voice came back to her. "You're saying I can be both?"

Astrid nodded. "Who you are is your choice and no one else's. Every day—every moment—you can decide who you are."

* * *

Greeta came awake to the sound of the guards dragging the stone back into place. It blocked out the bright sun. Diffused light hovered at the ceiling where it entered through the handholds.

"Greeta!" Frayka said. "Are you all right?"

"I'm fine," Greeta said when her friends helped her sit up. "I'm sorry. I thought I could get you out of here. I thought we could escape."

The dim light above allowed Greeta to

make out the shapes of her friends by her side.

"Don't be sorry," Frayka said. "We're together. That's a step in the right direction."

Greeta heard an edge in Frayka's voice, reminding her of their first day in the Land of Swamp Dragons when they met Jaya. "You were right," Greeta said. "We shouldn't have trusted the Swamp Landers. We should have defended ourselves against them."

Njall barked a bitter laugh. "Now we know they're dangerous and not to be trusted. It's a mistake we won't make again."

Greeta felt wretched and ashamed. "It's my fault. I should have been more careful."

"All you know is this country and its people," Frayka said. "How could you not be influenced by them?"

Greeta started when she felt Frayka's comforting hand on her shoulder.

"We are a different people," Frayka said. "Northlanders are nothing like the demons here in the Land of Vines."

Normally, Greeta would have corrected Frayka and told her the proper name was the Great Turtle Lands. Before today, Greeta would have flinched to hear Frayka call any native of the Great Turtle Lands a demon.

But after feeling welcomed in Xazaa, the Northlanders had experienced a rude awakening by being exiled from the city and brought to this one by guards.

Who knows what they plan to do with us? Will they make us their slaves? Will they kill us?

What if they are in league with Finehurst? Or what if his smoke dragon made the people of Xazaa believe we're to blame for the king's death? And what if this city is a place of punishment?

Until last year, Greeta had spent a quiet and happy life in her Shining Star village with Papa and Auntie Peppa. Now Greeta understood she'd lived a sheltered life, making her naïve and gullible.

Maybe that's what I wanted. Being naïve and gullible can make life easy and simple. My greatest problem was feeling rejected and unwanted by a man who probably never loved me. Now I worry about how to protect my people and possibly all of the Great Turtle Lands from a man who would harm them.

Greeta considered that being a native of the Shining Star nation gave her a quiet and peaceful life. Being a Northlander gave her a complicated and violent life.

It seemed to Greeta that the more complicated and violent life might allow her to be of greater service to the world.

But she couldn't be of service to anyone

trapped below ground.

"We have to find a way out of here," Greeta said. She pointed at the stone grate, far above her reach. "What if one of us climbs on Njall's shoulders? Maybe we can push the grate off."

"Tried that," Njall said. "Didn't work."

"There are tunnels all around us," Frayka said. "We've tried most of them. Each one leads to an opening to the outside. But the opening is so small you can only fit your arm through."

Greeta squinted but couldn't see much in the dark space. "I don't see any tunnels."

"Where we stand right now, it's like the hub of a wheel," Njall said. "Soon you'll be able to see the different tunnels splaying out in all directions." Turning to Frayka, he said, "We should keep trying. Maybe one of the tunnels will lead us out."

"It's pointless," Frayka said. "They all look the same."

"But we won't know until we try!" Njall said.

Greeta's vision became more adjusted to the dark. She realized she stood where Njall and Frayka had broken her fall. She gained her bearings.

The diffused light above shimmered and cast beams of light across the floor. Greeta recognized its smooth surface and white color. She crawled across it toward the nearest wall and saw dust from the white surface along the entire base of the wall.

Frayka paced. "Arguing won't get us out of here. I say we pick one direction and try it. Otherwise, there's no telling what the guards have in store for us the next time they come by."

When Greeta reached the wall, she picked up a handful of white dust. "I know what this is. I saw something like this in Xazaa." She showed the white dust to Frayka and Njall. "The Swamp Landers use this to make a paste they spread over stone surfaces. It allows them to catch and collect rain. The tunnels you found must be channels that send rain water to fields or containers."

A faint voice cried in the distance, echoing through one of the tunnels.

"What was that?" Greeta said.

"What?" Frayka said. "I heard nothing."

"Neither did I," Njall said.

The distant voice cried out again, more clearly this time.

"There!" Greeta said. "Someone is calling Finehurst's name."

"Not to my ears," Frayka said.

"Nor mine," Njall added.

Greeta's senses heightened. Her vision sharpened, and she saw the worried expressions on her friends' faces. She tuned in to the lingering echo. "That's Red Feather. I recognize his voice."

Her nose twitched at an unexpected acrid smell. "That's smoke," Greeta said. "Finehurst's smoke dragon must be here."

Before Frayka and Njall could argue, Greeta followed the scent of smoke into a tunnel and ran, still holding onto her handful of white dust.

RESA NELSON

CHAPTER 33

When flames blasted from the smoke dragon's mouth, Red Feather dropped to the floor. The leaves from the plant he carried covered his face. Red Feather panicked and tried to push them away until he recognized fresh air coming from their surface.

The plant. It's protecting me!

Red Feather thought back to a wall painting Jaya had shown him in her pyramid. Leaves thrown at the image of the smoke dragon in that painting had destroyed the creature. He reached back to touch the plant, and several leaves fell into his hand.

The flames filling the area subsided. Red Feather looked up to see the smoke dragon heaving as if it had run a great distance.

Jaya's dragons rolled on the floor, extinguishing bits of fire that danced across their scales.

Keeping a tight grip on the handful of leaves, Red Feather sprang forward until he came face-to-face with the smoke dragon. One by one, he held each leaf like a knife and hurled it into the smoke dragon.

Several thrown leaves struck the creature's surface and bounced off. But the final leaf pierced it.

The smoke dragon shrieked, and its voice carried surprise and disgust. The beast backed away from Red Feather.

Jaya's dragons took note of the creature's distress and charged toward it. The clatter of their claws against the stone ground filled the air.

A stem bearing many leaves tapped on Red Feather's shoulder. Looking back, he held up an empty hand, soon filled with those leaves. Before he could launch another attack, the smoke dragon sped down the passageway away from him.

Too late, Red Feather realized he had forgotten something: the words Jaya had so carefully taught him to say when fighting the smoke dragon.

The swamp dragons gave chase with Red Feather close behind.

The smoke dragon paused in a bright space lit by a cluster of firepots. It turned, preparing to breathe more fire.

One of Jaya's dragons jumped through the smoke dragon and circled it from the other side.

Surprised, the smoke dragon coughed a few short bursts of fire into the empty air. With Jaya's dragons snapping and lunging on either side, the smoke dragon trembled in alarm.

Catching up, Red Feather prepared to throw a leaf.

Seeing the threat, the smoke dragon smashed into the wall and disappeared into it.

Confused, Red Feather took a few steps closer. Within moments, he gained enough perspective to see a rising stairway illuminated by the many surrounding pots of fire.

The smoke dragon didn't disappear into the wall. It ran up this stairway!

"Finehurst!" Red Feather cried.

Keeping a firm grip on his handful of deadly leaves, Red Feather bolted up the stairs.

Jaya's swamp dragons bounded up the steps after him.

CHAPTER 34

Greeta ran through the tunnel in the darkness. Her vision had heightened to let her see the path ahead. She trailed her fingertips along one wall to keep her balance.

Behind, she heard Frayka and Njall arguing while they tried to keep up.

When a smaller tunnel branched off, Greeta shouted, "Stay in the main tunnel! Keep going straight!" She hoped her friends understood.

Red Feather's voice lingered in the air like the scent of roasted meat after a feast. The remnants of his voice acted like a beacon that Greeta followed.

Pale light appeared in the distance. Greeta ran toward it until she reached the end of the tunnel and an ascending stairway illuminated by a stone pot filled with fire. She paused and closed her eyes. Blocking out the sound of her friends' approaching footsteps, Greeta tilted one ear toward the stairway and listened for the lingering sound of Red Feather's voice.

Silence.

Frayka and Njall caught up and joined Greeta's side. Njall gazed up at the well lit but empty stairway. "Looks like we found our way out."

"We have to find Red Feather," Greeta said. "I heard his voice. And I still smell smoke. Finehurst's smoke dragon must be here."

Frayka took a deep breath. "I smell no smoke. But if the smoke dragon is here, we will destroy it once we find it. And if anyone gets in our way, we will fight. Agreed?"

Greeta nodded. She regretted having given her trust so quickly and easily to Jaya and other Swamp Landers. Her own Shining Star village had never treated visitors with the irreverence Greeta and the other Northlanders experienced here. She saw no reason to disagree with Frayka anymore. "Agreed."

"Wait," Njall said. He leaned down to examine the fire pot. Njall pulled out a long carved stone and handed the cool end to Greeta. "Looks like a fire rake. We have our daggers. Your sword is still in Xazaa. This should help."

Greeta examined the carved stone. Roughly the size and shape of a short sword, it fit neatly in her free hand. She sensed heat coming from its blackened point, used to the stir the fire. She nodded her thanks to Njall and led the way up the steps.

When they arrived at a square landing, Frayka said, "We should be above ground by now."

Njall said, "Do you see any way outside? All I see are stone walls around us and steps leading below and above."

"We must be inside the pyramid," Greeta said.

The shouts of guards echoed in the tunnel below.

Greeta hurried up the stairway and its jagged path with Frayka and Njall behind her. They discovered landing after landing. At last, the stairway opened up into a large room surrounded by slanted walls.

Several painted priestesses sat circled around a cluster of candles in the center of the room. The candles illuminated a small model of the Xazaa pyramid opposite a model of the pyramid that they now inhabited.

While the others chanted, the priestess with the yellow skin moved an effigy of a dragon from the top of the Xazaa pyramid to the other pyramid. A bundle of dried sage burned in a large seashell. Yellow

Skin waved the smoke curling from the sage all around the dragon effigy.

"She's calling Finehurst to her," Greeta said. "She's working with Finehurst!"

The priestesses turned to look at Greeta.

"Kaypahl!" one of the seated priestesses shouted at the yellow-skinned woman.

Frayka and Njall clasped their daggers and stood on either side of the circled priestesses, forcing them to stay seated.

"We have to kill them!" Frayka said.

"Kaypahl," Greeta repeated, glaring into the priestess's eyes. "This time we show no mercy."

Lunging forward, Greeta stabbed at the woman but missed when Kaypahl dropped to her knees.

Wide-eyed with confusion, Kaypahl stared at Greeta and held out her empty hands to show she was unarmed.

Do not make my mistake.

Greeta recognized the sound of Margreet's voice in her head. She knew the ghost woman had once said these same words to her either in this reality or the Dreamtime. Greeta couldn't remember which. Or what those words meant.

Shaking off the voice in her head, Greeta steeled herself. She and her friends had to fight to escape and survive. The Swamp Landers gave them no other choice. She raised her stone sword, preparing to strike.

"Red Feather!" Kaypahl said.

Greeta stopped herself with the stone sword in mid-air. "What?"

Seizing the opportunity, Kaypahl said, "Red Feather! Red Feather!" She pointed at the shadowed walls surrounding them.

Greeta sank to her knees and held the sharp edge of the carved stone next to Kaypahl's throat. "Where is he? What do you know about Red Feather?"

One of the other women from the circle stood and said, "Greeta." White paint decorated with small brown dots covered her skin. Minus the large headdress of small white flowers and thick leafy vines, she looked the same as the day the Northlanders first met her.

"Jaya!" Greeta said.

But before Greeta could decide what to do next, the opposite side of the room filled with black smoke that took the shape of a dragon.

CHAPTER 35

When the smoke dragon materialized, the priestesses still seated in the center of the room joined hands and chanted in unison. The candle flames they surrounded flickered, casting distorted shadows around the room.

Frayka and Njall charged at the creature. Forgetting her desire to kill the yellow-skinned priestess and possibly Jaya, Greeta rushed to fight alongside the Northlanders.

Kaypahl and Jaya resumed their places in the circle of priestesses and joined them in chanting.

Soft light smoldered behind and through the smoke dragon. Its outline appeared sharp, but the smoke within looked ethereal, constantly twisting and turning. The beast's eyes burned bright. Its head swung from side to side as if searching for something.

Njall charged the smoke dragon, slashed it with his dagger, and then retreated to safety.

The dagger blow created a gaping wound of air and light, but the wound immediately sealed itself. The smoke dragon hissed at Njall and stomped its foot, making the room shudder.

The chanting grew louder, and the priestesses' voices reverberated throughout the room.

On Greeta's signal, all of the Northlanders charged and slashed at the smoke dragon. But when their weapons sliced through the creature, it stepped through them so that each open wound passed around the Northlander responsible for making it.

When the smoke moved around and above Greeta, she caught her breath. She turned and saw the smoke dragon face the priestesses.

The sudden sense of cold sent shock waves through her body. Fear swept through Greeta as if she'd fallen overboard into the ocean from a ship that now vanished on the horizon. She felt alone and lost at sea.

Wisps of black smoke curled around her. Greeta struggled to breathe, feeling deserted and hopeless.

A small, thin object whizzed past her face and through the body of smoke, leaving it unharmed.

She heard a man saying the same few words in the Swamp Lander language over and over again: "Uht vuu sway! Uht vuu sway!"

Red Feather!

Greeta recognized his voice even though she didn't understand his words. Another object flew past her. This time she recognized it as a leaf.

It also fell uselessly through the smoke dragon, which became thicker and more defined.

"Jaya!" Red Feather's voice cried. "It isn't working!"

Suddenly, Greeta realized she still held onto a fist full of white dust. She remembered what she'd seen Astrid do in the Dreamtime. And the advice her mother had given.

Now is the moment for me to be a Northlander.

Greeta faced the smoke dragon and paced toward it.

The creature's smoky tail wrapped around Greeta and lifted her into the air.

Feeling the creature squeeze her chest so tight that she couldn't breathe, Greeta threw the white dust at it.

The dust absorbed light and glowed bright white. The light surrounded the smoke dragon and held it still.

Greeta tried shouting to Red Feather, but the tail squeezing her chest made it impossible.

Stepping into sight, Red Feather threw another leaf with all his might.

This time, the leaf impaled the smoke dragon and caused a gaping wound. A beam of white dusty light streamed into that wound.

The smoke dragon cried out in pain and whipped its head back toward the Northlanders.

The wisps of smoke bound Greeta with despair and blinded her with sorrow.

More whizzing sounds pierced the air. More leaves impaled the creature, leaving wounds that the white light then penetrated.

Each time, the smoke dragon bellowed in protest.

Suddenly, the wisps darted away from Greeta and the creature's tail released her. Falling into a heap on the ground, she took a gasp of freedom.

The women's chanting turned to rhythmic shouts.

Writhing in pain, the smoke dragon wheezed pitiful fire onto the stone floor. The flames illuminated the surrounding walls, filled with images. Many wisps of smoke circled the perimeter of the room and skimmed across each decorated wall.

The wisps entwined and darted down the stairway where the Northlanders had entered.

The smoke dragon exploded into gray dust that settled on the floor.

Finehurst may not be dead, Greeta thought. *But at least this part of him is gone.*

The chanting ceased, and the priestesses studied the dust while Jaya stepped forward, smiling. "Chaca," she said. "Zolten."

The two swamp dragons shouldered their way past Greeta and jumped happily at Jaya's feet.

Sensing another presence behind her, Greeta turned.

A weary Red Feather smiled. "Hello, Greeta."

CHAPTER 36

Happy and relieved to see Red Feather, Greeta ran to embrace him. She said, "I don't understand. How did you get here? How did you find us?"

Red Feather stepped away and removed an unlit torch from a sconce, walked toward the priestesses' candles, and used them to give flame to the torch. He walked along the walls, giving light to the decorations. Red Feather stopped and gestured for Greeta to join him. "This is how I got here."

Joining his side, Greeta looked at the wall and realized they didn't bear decorations. Instead, they were covered with illustrations of events.

"I saw these same illustrations inside the pyramid at Xazaa." Red Feather pointed to a scene that showed the smoke dragon at the pyramid of Xazaa. The next picture showed a warrior climbing out of the mouth of the serpent shadow crawling down the pyramid. He cleared his throat. "That would be me."

Frayka stood behind Red Feather. She pointed over his shoulder at the warrior climbing out of the serpent's mouth. "What is that supposed to be?"

"It's him," Greeta said. She gestured toward Red Feather.

Frayka snorted. "It looks nothing like him."

"That is a Swamp Lander," Njall added. "The little man is not a Swamp Lander."

"What do they say?" Red Feather asked Greeta.

"You don't want to know," Greeta said. She examined the following scenes. The appearance of monsters attacking the warrior startled her. Turning to Red Feather, she said, "Did you do these things?"

"The swamp dragons helped." He shrugged. "In a manner of speaking." Red Feather pointed at an image on the far right. "This is how I found you. Jaya showed me the same wall of pictures in the Xazaa pyramid."

"The Xazaa pyramid?" Greeta said. "Why would the royal family allow Jaya inside the pyramid?"

Ignoring her question, Red Feather repeated, "This is how I found you."

Greeta looked at where he pointed but the picture she saw confused her. A lone blonde woman with fair skin stood, casting a long shadow in front of a tapestry that looked a great deal like Finehurst's tapestry.

"Oh, look!" Frayka said, now pointing at the same image. "It's Greeta!"

CHAPTER 37

Greeta's head swam for the rest of the day. She'd learned too much too fast. Information buzzed around her like a swarm of annoying gnats.

That evening the Northlanders joined a feast inside the temple, now sitting among the priestesses who had imprisoned them. Red Feather listened intently while Jaya and Kaypahl spoke simple Swamp Lander words to him. They paused every so often to give him time to translate for Greeta.

"I think they're saying there have been legends of their gods helping your gods for generations," Red Feather said. "The legend is about a Northlander woman who must learn from the people of the Great Turtle Lands and use that knowledge to help the Northlands."

Greeta felt lost in a sea of confusion.

I almost killed an innocent woman because I let unjustified rage get the better of me. Is that the cost of being a Northlander?

Red Feather continued. "But they had to make sure you're the right one. Or that you're worthy. Or something along those lines."

Frayka propped her elbows on the tabletop and chewed on a roasted chicken leg. "What does the little man say? Why is Jaya here?"

"I told you already." Greeta reminded herself that Frayka and Njall were likely to be as frazzled as she felt. "Jaya is the king's daughter."

"The dead king," Njall said. "The one killed by the smoke dragon."

"That's the one," Greeta said. "Red Feather believes that Jaya is his oldest child. I think that's why she's king now. She told Red Feather to find me here."

Njall nudged Frayka. "Notice how Jaya failed to tell the little man to look for *us* while he happened to be in the vicinity!"

After listening to the priestess and the new king further, Red Feather turned to Greeta. Looking startled, he stared at her. "What's wrong?"

"Nothing," Greeta said too brightly.

When I decide to be a Northlander, can Red Feather love me? Wouldn't he rather love a woman who is wholly and completely a member of the Shining Star nation like him?

Or could he love someone who is sometimes a Northlander and sometimes a Shining Star woman?

Greeta pushed at her food but didn't eat it. "What does Jaya say now?"

Red Feather looked at her in silence.

Greeta reminded herself that as long as she spoke the Shining Star language, only Red Feather would understand her. She didn't want anyone but him to know her thoughts. "I almost killed that woman talking to Jaya. The one whose skin is painted yellow. I would have killed her if you hadn't come into the room."

His eyebrows twisted in confusion. "Why?"

"I thought we were in danger. I thought they might kill us if we didn't kill them first."

Red Feather looked even more confused. "But these are Swamp Landers. Their nation is part of the Great Turtle Lands. They're our people. Our blood."

"Yours," Greeta said. "Look at me. I look like the Northlanders. I *am* a Northlander. Why wouldn't the Swamp Landers want to kill me?"

"Because they believe in the seven generations," Red Feather said. "Like us, they consider how their actions will affect the next seven generations before taking any action."

Like us.

Red Feather's words gave Greeta a glimmer of hope.

Greeta glanced at Frayka and Njall, now deep in conversation themselves. She focused on keeping her composure to avoid drawing their attention. "That's what I failed to do. I forgot about the seven generations. I forgot everything I learned from the Shining Star nation."

By the way Red Feather followed her gaze at the other Northlanders, Greeta suspected he appreciated the sensitivity of her words. "What happened," Red Feather said, "that made you forget?"

"I was fine when we arrived in the Land of Swamp Dragons," Greeta said. "I intended to track down Finehurst and stop him from hurting more people. But things began to change when we met Jaya." Greeta paused, mindful of the words she chose. If she mentioned Frayka or Njall by name, they'd wonder what Greeta said about them. "My friends thought we were in danger and should kill Jaya."

"But you did not," Red Feather said. "And you convinced them that you could befriend her."

Greeta nodded. "And after we arrived in the city and found you, everything seemed fine. But it changed yesterday afternoon. We were thrown out of the city. The guards pointed weapons at us and brought us here."

"Perhaps the Swamp Landers had the same misgivings about you that you had about them."

Red Feather's words resonated with Greeta. Had they all simply reached a point where they felt so afraid of each other that they lost sight of the true enemy?

"Ever since I left the Shining Star nation, my new friends have told me I'm too soft hearted. Even you agreed with them once. They think I should be more fierce and aggressive like they are."

Red Feather looked at her steadily. "Are you saying what happened is their fault?"

"No," Greeta said. "I think they're right. Maybe I am too soft hearted and need to become more like a warrior. But it was my decision to hold a weapon against that woman's throat. Not theirs. I never should have done it. I thought all the wrong things about these people, and I could have committed murder. How could I live with myself if I killed someone?"

"But you didn't." Red Feather looked up when Jaya tapped his shoulder. He made a graceful gesture as if asking her to wait. Turning back to Greeta, he said, "And perhaps because of this experience, you will never make such a rash decision again."

Red Feather then gave his attention to Jaya and listened to her.

When Greeta made another attempt to eat her dinner, she found Frayka and Njall staring at her.

"That seemed quite a conversation," Frayka said.

Njall raised an eyebrow. "What did the little man have to say?"

"It's personal," Greeta said. She sat up straight and met their gazes. "It's about how I disappointed myself."

Frayka and Njall exchanged glances and laughed.

"Don't be so hard on yourself," Frayka said. She stabbed a chunk of roasted chicken with her own dagger and then handed the grip to Greeta. "You'll feel better if you eat something."

Greeta smiled and took a bite.

The conversation between Jaya, the priestess, and Red Feather grew louder.

"Wait," Red Feather said to the Swamp Landers. "I don't understand."

"Oh, look!" Frayka said, delighted. "They're acting something out." Nudging Njall, she said, "Let's play along."

Jaya pushed away the last bits of her meal away from the tabletop in front on her. She rested her head on it, pillowed by her arms.

"She's taking a nap," Njall said.

"She's tired," Frayka guessed.

"She's dead," Njall said.

Frayka scrunched up her nose and

pointed at Jaya. "Look at the way she rests her head on her folded arms. You don't do that when you're dead."

"I don't understand," Red Feather said to Greeta. "What are Njall and Frayka doing?"

"Don't mind them," Greeta said. "But what do you think Jaya is doing?"

"Trying to tell me something," Red Feather said. "But she baffles me."

Jaya pulled a small bench behind Greeta. Jaya pointed at Greeta and gestured at the empty wall behind her.

"She wants Greeta to climb over the bench and stand by the wall," Njall guessed.

"I don't think so." Frayka brightened. "She's talking about the picture we saw on the wall inside the pyramid. The one showing Greeta!"

Greeta shook her head. "I doubt it." She struggled with the idea that she appeared in the picture, no matter what stories Red Feather told about how he knew where to find her. It could have been any North-lander woman on that wall painting.

Jaya climbed on top of the bench she'd placed behind Greeta and stood with her shoulders back and her fists on her hips.

Njall turned to Frayka. "I have no idea what that means," he said.

"You give up too easily," Frayka said. She peered intently at Jaya. "Look how she stands behind Greeta. That must mean something."

"Does she pretend to be a mountain?" Njall said to Greeta, "Ask your little man if Jaya speaks of mountains."

Greeta's first thought was to say no one understood what Jaya meant. But then she realized that sharing their thoughts might help them all understand Jaya. She relayed Njall's question.

"I don't know about mountains," Red Feather told Greeta. "But Jaya was this insistent when she showed me that I needed to come here. Maybe she thinks there's a place we need to go. Maybe the reason is in the painting we saw but we don't recognize that reason yet."

Greeta translated Red Feather's answer for the Northlanders and then strained to remember the details of the painting.

Jaya raised her hands high above her head.

"She wants to touch the sky," Njall said. "She wants to be a bird and fly away."

"She stands tall," Frayka guessed. "She wants to be tall like a Northlander."

"No, taller." Njall slammed his hand on the tabletop in triumph. "I've got it! Who stands taller than Northlanders? There is only one answer. She wants to be a giant."

"Yes!" Excited, Frayka pointed at where Jaya had been sitting. "But there is more, remember? She rested her head there before."

"She wants to kill giants!" Njall said.

"Nonsense," Frayka said. "She wants to help giants take a nap."

Greeta snapped out of her own thoughts. The Northlanders' conversation made her think of stories she'd heard long ago in her Shining Star nation home. Stories of other nations in the Great Turtle Lands. "The Land of Sleeping Giants," she said to Red Feather.

He slumped in relief. "Yes. That must be what she means. But why would Jaya want us to go there? The Land of Sleeping Giants is to the far west."

Greeta remembered one detail of the painting that now seemed critical.

The image of the Northlander woman had cast a long shadow.

"I think," Greeta said, "that's where we'll find Shadow. And if Shadow has gone to the Land of Sleeping Giants, it must be for a good reason."

Red Feather nodded. "Do you think it has something to do with Finehurst?"

"Most likely," Greeta said. "Shadow walks in the Dreamtime. She sees things most people never see. Shadow knows about things that are destined to happen. She may have found him."

"And if we find Shadow," Red Feather said, "we find Finehurst."

CHAPTER 38

After traveling back to Xazaa with Jaya and her guards, Greeta and her friends returned to Red Feather's temple to prepare for the journey ahead. Frayka and Njall helped Red Feather collect herbs and plants. He also checked their dragon bite wounds and redressed them.

Greeta reclaimed her sword.

After hearing Red Feather's story about the city kings in the Land of Swamp Dragons and how Jaya might soon be at risk of being attacked, Greeta spent a day showing Jaya how to fight. Greeta discovered that a spear worked just as well as a sword. With Red Feather's help, she convinced Jaya to make pictures of what Greeta taught and practice every day.

When they prepared to leave the city, Jaya met them at the base of the pyramid.

She looked the same as when they first
met, wearing white paint covered with
small, brown dots and a towering headdress of greenery and flowers. The swamp
dragons flanked her. They curled their
tails around her feet.

Briefly, Jaya embraced Greeta.

Greeta felt uncomfortable, thinking
about what might have been if she'd made
other decisions.

*What if I'd listened to Njall and Frayka
and killed Jaya on the day we met her?
She wouldn't have been here to show Red
Feather how to find me. Someone else in
her family might have become king. What
would have happened to us then?*

Greeta shifted her weight from one foot
to the other, unable to find comfort in the
way she stood.

*I almost killed a priestess. If Jaya and
Red Feather hadn't been there, I would
have done it. I'd be a murderer now. What
would have happened next? Would we
have slaughtered all of the priestesses?*

*Is that what Finehurst wanted? Did he
lead us to the Land of Swamp Dragons
hoping we'd kill people and never find out
they had a prophecy about me? Or did he
not know that their gods agreed to help the
Northlander gods long ago?*

Greeta made a silent promise to herself
that she would never forget the seven generations again.

Red Feather stepped forward to face Jaya and held out the plant whose leaves he'd used to defeat the smoke dragon. "This belongs to your family."

Smiling, Jaya took the plant from him and placed it on the ground. The swamp dragons sniffed and inspected it. The leaves shuddered in response.

Speaking words Greeta didn't understand, Jaya embraced Red Feather.

A new concern swept through Greeta's veins. Watching the embracing couple, she worried. Was Jaya inviting Red Feather to stay in Xazaa? Did he want to live here?

Greeta swallowed the lump in her throat.

What if I never see him again?

Releasing Red Feather, Jaya clapped her hands on his shoulders. She then handed the plant back to him. Beaming, she walked up the pyramid steps.

The swamp dragons stayed behind and nosed Red Feather's feet.

Greeta raised an eyebrow at Red Feather.

Cradling the plant in his arms, Red Feather said, "Let's go."

* * *

Greeta, Red Feather, and the Northlanders returned to the ship they'd hidden on the beach. However, they found it standing in the open.

The dead man Erik stood on deck and looked down at them. "Well," he announced. "Look what the swamp dragon dragged in."

Antoni and many other dead men emerged from below deck.

Greeta smiled at them. "What happened? How did you get here?"

Erik jumped from the ship onto the sand. He strolled toward Greeta. "After getting kicked out of the swamp, there wasn't much other choice than to retrace our steps." Erik gave a nod toward Antoni, who joined his side.

Smiling, Antoni said, "Good to see you all survived."

Erik smacked Antoni's arm so hard that the dead man's rocky elbow fell off. "Despite the way you let that woman and her dragons tell us we're not good enough for the likes of the Swamp Landers, we made ourselves useful. So we retraced our steps, found the bits and pieces of our friends in the wreckage of Finehurst's ice ship, and put them back together again."

"More or less," Antoni added.

"And now we're ready to go home," Erik said.

"We can't go back to the Land of Ice yet," Greeta said. "We've agreed to sail to the Land of Sleeping Giants."

"That doesn't sound at all safe," Antoni said. "If there are giants, what happens if they wake up?"

Erik nodded. "Antoni's right. We've all been through enough."

"It's not your decision to make," Njall said. "Our people built this ship. It belongs to us, not you."

Erik laughed. "But there's more of us than you."

Frayka rested her arm on Njall's shoulder. "There's talk of Finehurst being in the Land of Sleeping Giants."

"Oh." Erik brightened. "Why didn't you say so in the first place? There's always time for vengeance."

Greeta stood on the sand and stared at the ocean while the Northlanders boarded the ship.

"Are you coming with us?" Red Feather said. He smiled when he joined her side.

Greeta swallowed hard. While she appreciated her mother's advice, Greeta still struggled to understand how to take it. "I don't know what I am."

Perplexed, Red Feather frowned. "You are Greeta."

"Part of me belongs to the Shining Star nation," Greeta said. "But I'm a Northlander, too. And people of the Northlands are the opposite of Shining Star people. Northlanders are fierce warriors who don't hesitate to kill. Shining Star people are peaceful. How can I be both?"

Red Feather stood so close that his arm

grazed hers.

Greeta caught her breath at the touch of his skin.

"Perhaps that is why you can't control becoming a dragon," Red Feather said. "It seems to me that most shapeshifters are at ease in their own skins. I've heard that helps them take different shapes. Their outside appearance changes because they know how to keep what's inside them the same."

"But how do I learn how to be at ease when I feel at war with myself?" Greeta whispered.

Red Feather shrugged. "Perhaps it's possible to be a warrior when needed and a peacemaker when needed. You've got plenty of Northlanders to help you be a warrior. And if you need reminding of how to be peaceful, you've got me."

He walked toward the ship. The swamp dragons trotted to greet him and then lumbered up a plank to board the ship. "The others are ready. Are you?"

"Yes," Greeta said. The peaceful sense of being a member of the Shining Star nation returned to her for the first time since arriving in the Land of Swamp Dragons. "I think so."

CHAPTER 39

Finehurst stretched awake on the bed in his Shining Star mansion when something light and airy tickled his nose. When he tried to brush it away, his hand passed through it.

Suddenly wide awake, he sat up in bed to face a small and wispy dragon made of black smoke. He pieced together what this unexpected turn of events meant.

The only time he'd set up this type of magic happened 20 years ago when he'd captured that water goddess bitch and imprisoned her in ice. The boy alchemist employed by Finehurst had predicted she was the only god with close enough ties to challenge one's ability to travel on any waterway.

But if she'd been released recently, the magic he'd established would have materialized in Finehurst's own image.

Finehurst struggled to remember the series of safeguards he'd created. The release of the goddess and the destruction of her ice castle prison should have triggered a reflection of himself to follow the instructions he'd set in place. If pursued, his image would have created a ship from the ice castle ruins and drawn any attackers out to sea. If the attack persisted, Finehurst's double would draw those who threatened it to a place most likely to destroy them.

He knew what the appearance of this pitiful excuse of a smoke dragon meant.

Decades ago, a girl stole away his livelyhood in the Northlands by claiming her position as the blacksmith of Guell. She ruined his life.

The boy alchemist told Finehurst how to set up magic to defeat her should that Northlander woman ever get in his way again. But if the attempts to defeat her should fail, any remnants of the smoke dragon would come to warn Finehurst.

"Astrid." Finehurst spit the name out in disgust.

Who else could it be? Who else could have caused everything to go so wrong in the Land of Ice?

The smoke dragon hovered in the air before him and rearranged itself to show him a picture of an arid land, Finehurst standing among peculiar formations, and beings much larger than mortals lying among them.

After being chased out of his home in the Shining Star nation, Finehurst had returned to it after making certain the pesky Greeta had vanished.

Although he'd spent most of his life here in the Shining Star nation, he had traveled throughout the Great Turtle Lands in his earlier years. He'd encountered many nations and learned of others. For that reason, he recognized what the smoke showed him.

"The Land of Sleeping Giants," Finehurst said.

The smoke reconfigured itself into the shape of a dragon, which opened its jaws and roared at him. The smoke dragon then exploded, and flakes of slag drifted down on Finehurst and his bed.

"What a mess!" Finehurst shouted. Enraged, he jumped out of bed and brushed away the flakes of slag. He trembled with anger.

He understood every bit of information the smoke dragon brought to him. This could only mean that horrible Astrid still lived and now made her way to the Land of Sleeping Giants.

Finehurst shuddered when he thought of what could happen if she arrived there first. He raced through his mansion and toward the ship he kept in the lake below. It would be risky to travel by water, but he banked on the chance that it would take a good long while for the water goddess to find him.

The slag shimmered and transformed into threads that wove themselves into a strip torn from a tapestry.

Finehurst picked up the piece of tapestry from the floor and examined it.

He had to hurry and take every risk in order to prevent his well laid plans from falling apart before he could execute them and establish himself as the ruler of all the Great Turtle Lands.

ABOUT THE AUTHOR

When Resa Nelson's short story "The Dragonslayer's Sword" was first published in *Science Fiction Age* magazine, it ranked 2nd in that magazine's first Readers Top Ten poll. Around the same time, the manager of a major bookstore contacted the magazine editor asking how to buy the novel because many of his customers were asking to buy it.

No such novel existed. Only the short story existed. Readers assumed it had come from a novel.

This is when Resa realized all her readers are smarter than she is, because they knew there was more to the story. It only took her eight years to figure out what they already knew. She plans to write at least four series that take place in her Dragonslayer World. Series #1 (Dragonslayer Series) is complete. *Dragonfly* is Book 1 in the Dragonfly series.

Visit Resa's website at www.resanelson.com and follow her on Twitter at @ResaNelson.

Look for the final book in the Dragonfly
series to be published by Fall 2016.

For notifications of new releases by
Resa Nelson, sign up at her website:

www.resanelson.com

Made in the USA
Las Vegas, NV
25 July 2021

27007441R10174